THE
ADVENTURES
OF
JULES KHAN

A Teenage Muslim Superhero

by

KARIM K DEVJI

THE ADVENTURES OF
JULES KHAN

⚡

A Teenage
Muslim Superhero

By

Karim K Devji

The Adventures of Jules Khan ©
Written, Produced and Created by Karim Kassamali Devji

Published by: Karim K Devji,
Burnaby, British Columbia,
Canada V5A 4V4
www.juleskhan.com

© 2018 Karim K Devji

2nd Edition,
Edition number 786110/03-08-18
3rd August 2018

For official and legal permissions contact:
Pluralism7@gmail.com

ISBN: 978-1-9993805-4-0 (Audio)
ISBN: 978-1-9993805-3-3 (Paperback)
ISBN: 978-1-9993805-2-6 (Hardcover book)
ISBN: 978-1-9993805-1-9 (Electronic book)
ISBN: 978-1-9993805-0-2 (Book)

Library and Archives, Government of Canada

Future offices located in:

New York City,
New York,
United States of America

Dedication

I dedicate this book to my children, Mehreen and Ahmad, to my dear wife, my sister and my amazing mother and my brilliant father, who have supported me throughout this journey, and to all the amazing children that

Live on earth

Today and tomorrow.

It is our duty as adults to leave

This earth in a

Better state then we found it.

Smile!

Acknowledgments

A humble thank you to
my dear family,
friends and

anyone who

helps with developing
'The Adventures of Jules Khan'

journey; from the editors,

to the graphics,

to the religions and to the people
I meet throughout

my life.

Thank you all

(Shukhran)

x

Contents

1

The King

"SMILE," THE PHOTOGRAPHER requested, before he took the customary wedding photos. The Royal Orchestra played Louis Armstrong's jazz pieces, and sunshine flowed everywhere; all the guests were dancing, singing and being merry.

It was a beautiful, sunny, crisp September 7th, 1925. My parents were married in the South of France by a young Persian prince who lived in Europe and soon after was crowned King of the Refugees. They called him His Holiness Rumi Khan. He was rumored to be an intellectual, mystical king, and he was everything you would not expect from a king. He was more European-looking than Indian or Persian looking, as he was born from a Swedish mother and a Persian father. This new-age king was as handsome, wealthy, wise, humble and eloquent as they came. He made his fortune through investments in the stock market and through developing something called Bits of Coin, or what he called a futuristic new currency based on algorithms discovered in the 7th Century in Persia. "No one believes in the new currency, but in time, there will be no such thing as money!" he proclaimed. This king was transparent with his wealth, as he never stole from his own people like most monarchs, religions or governments do.

This particular king did not fit the profile of any king I know of. He was a prince that inherited his father's problems; he did not inherit wealth, fortune or buildings, and on top of this, he inherited a loyal yet disorganized set of followers. However, slowly but surely, through the process of an Eastern and Western education, this prince who became king transformed his once-tattered community into one of the most sophisticated, wealthy and intelligent communities on the planet. With his success came responsibility, and eventually word spread in many countries that

King Rumi would be able to figure out solutions for global refugees to settle down in the Western world. Of course, no human being on this planet wants to be saddled with another person, but King Rumi had inherited the responsibility of thousands of refugees, and to live with this feeling every day must have been burdensome and overwhelming for the king.

However, this king seemed to be blessed with some sort of divinity, because he constantly smiled, joked and laughed all the time while working 18 hours a day for his community and humanity. He was as humble as Mother Teresa and Mahatma Gandhi, and he listened to his followers as opposed to ordering them around. King Rumi's popularity spread throughout Europe; world leaders, nobles and even regular people would seek his advice on how to settle refugees of their own country regardless of faith or race.

Hi there! My name is Jules, Jules Khan, and yes, I am the main character of this story. I am a blonde-haired, blue- and green-eyed athletic teenager endowed with Superhero powers. I will try my best to narrate this exciting adventure as best I can, but bear with me and my immaturity; I am only a teenager!

I was told that my parents held their wedding in King Rumi's Palace with hundreds of dignitaries and famous people attending, as well as infamous people who just happened to be passing by! Everyone joined in the wedding, and I was told there was dancing, singing, eating and drinking. No alcohol was served, as both my parents do not drink alcohol; their choice, I guess.

The king's words to my parents when he was the officiant at their wedding ceremony went something like this: "Work hard for your children; work hard for their children and their children's children."

Wow, that will teach any king to learn how to use a bird's-eye view all the time!

The king was heavily involved in intellectual research and would request the presence of my mum and dad on many occasions. It even felt as if we were related, as we were secretly brought to his Palace so many times. Any time we were at the Palace, I would always sneak into the royal library, and I would love the feeling of all the old books that were there.

My mum came from royalty. She was born into an elite class of Jewish families. Her family business was custom tailoring for the rich and famous. My mother's family were immigrants from Sweden. Her parents were excellent with their hands, and as more and more Jewish refugees poured into Sweden, her parents decided to create shelters made from tarps. They made tents that were so durable that they decided to open up a custom tailoring business for tarps, tents and clothing. Well, the tent business thrived for a few years, but the custom clothing took off like hot cakes. They decided to move to Monaco, in the South of France, as they had customers from France who convinced them that French elites would start throwing money at them for their custom tailoring. Before you know it, my mum's family's business took off in France!

World War One had just ended a few years ago, and the world had witnessed a colossal loss of life; many families started to think about protecting their loved ones. My mum's family, on the other hand, was proactive and had ingeniously figured out how to prevent rain drops, snow and ice from penetrating the tarps for the benefit of the soldiers and the general public. This then extended to ingeniously figuring out how to make protective clothing; more specifically, making everyday clothing bullet- and shrapnel-proof in case another World War broke out. My mum's family studied the silk material patterns from spider webs and how the webs would disperse impact and absorb incoming flying objects, such as flies, without breaking the complexity of the delicate web. With this discovery, my mum invented a process by using delicate, thread-like layers of melted titanium string using the same web variations and then stitching and integrating the titanium into the weaves of wool and silk in the clothing. Then, voila! A trademark bullet- and shrapnel-proof clothing invention! My mum's family could not keep up with the demand for their custom protective clothing.

When I was 5 years old, one of my memories was watching my Mum shoot holes into my dad's clothing – of course, he was not at home! I always thought this was where polka dots came from!

I asked her, "Mama, is that how you make polka dots?"

"No, Jules, I am trying to see how to protect people from bullets."

"Mama, are bullets jelly beans?"

"No, Jules, they are metal pieces thrown at very high speeds."

"Mama, are they candies that you are throwing?"

"Jules, these are not sweets I am dealing with. Did you want a candy?"

"Yes, mama. Can I have as many candies as the holes in papa's shirt?"

My mum burst out laughing; she knew I just wanted to drown in candies!

"No, Jules, you cannot. Please get back in the house and color or paint."

"Mama, please give me candy and tell me a story. I am tired of painting polka dots on papa's shirts!"

My mum laughed and laughed. That was my first memory of my mum laughing so much!

Yes, I did get all the candies I wanted, and sure enough, my mum figured out a way to protect people with her innovative clothing line.

My mum had stitched the elites' formal apparel worth thousands of francs in a matter of a few months. She learned how to design and stitch technically-advanced clothing materials, and her specialty was stitching light, 100% wool, silk and titanium, weather-resistant, bullet- and shrapnel-proof men's, women's and children's bespoke suits. She figured that, one day, the world would go into war again, and what better items to protect you than your own daily high-end clothing?

My dad, on the other hand, was born in India in desperate poverty. His father's side (my grandfather) had originally immigrated from Persia to India in search of a safer life. My grandmother was from Greece, and he kept on telling me she was a descendant of Alexander the Great! What a joker! My dad, though, belonged to a faith of peace; he was taught to be kind, intelligent, nice, disciplined and humble. He was taught to treat his parents as divine, to look after others, to be caring and to realize his place on earth. He was taught to love and trust in God, to serve God with humility, and to accept and respect all devotional beliefs. He was also taught to be super ambitious, as long as he was ethical, and to share his wealth with his family, friends and those less fortunate. My dad's parents were so poor that they only ate one meal a day. The rest of the time, they kept on saving whatever they had and sent my dad to a Christian Church School in India. There, he learned how to read, speak and write English at a very proficient level. My dad's family got a lucky break when his own parents were employees of a Swedish water engineer living in India. As time went by, my dad started working for the same Swedish water engineering firm, where he found a position in one of the hydro dams as a translator.

Slowly but surely, my dad also began saving his salary and decided to leave for better economic prospects in the United Kingdom. He waved goodbye to his friends and boarded the steam ship with his parents; they entered the 3rd class cabins and never looked back. As the ship stopped for refueling in Spain for a week, the family decided to take a trip to the South of France, as my dad had always wanted to visit Monaco. He purchased tickets for him and my grandparents from quite the character to sail everyone back and forth to Monaco. They all gasped when the sailboat pulled into Monaco harbor; it was beautiful, they said, and all they had to do was look for accommodation. My dad loved what he saw in this beautiful town: the beautiful architecture, small roads and great-smelling breads! As he began walking towards the town, he came across a boutique clothing store. He gently pushed the door open, and the bell swung and rang. As he entered, he saw an older gentleman stitching clothes, an older lady organizing some shiny thread, and a beautiful young lady who was sitting behind a desk.

As he looked around and moved closer to the young lady, who was busy drawing designs, he found the courage to speak.

"Excuse me, kind lady, may I have your permission to browse your magnificent boutique and have a look around?" he eloquently asked.

"Why, kind sir, of course you may. We have suits for men, women and children; if you need any assistance, we will be here to help you," the woman replied.

My dad fell in love in that moment; her beautiful blonde hair and green eyes made him swoon. My mum could not keep her eyes off this unique-looking man either, I was told.

My dad started speaking to the young sales

lady. "I am travelling to England, and I understand the English are quite dapper, so I am in need of a suit that would make me look a little grown up and hopefully make me feel important," he started.

"Well, kind sir, since you seem to be from a far-away land, should it not be the English who should dress for you?" she responded.

My father laughed and said, "Indeed, I agree. I do find Monaco as romantic as it is portrayed in the many books I have read!"

"Romance can happen anywhere, at any time," she replied.

"My kind lady, I have to be honest with you: ever since I walked into this boutique, I cannot seem to see anything but you and your smile. May I have a kind word with your parents before I begin to embarrass my good self?" he asked.

"Absolutely. Mama, Papa…may I introduce you to my future?" was her answer.

They fell in love at first sight, and between them, the rest was history.

My dad decided to live in France if he wanted to marry my mum. He eventually found work as an insurance salesman and then rose to fame and fortune by working as an insurance clerk in Paris. Then, on a pure, uncalculated risk, he purchased an Italian restaurant called Lavarini's whose owner was leaving for Italy. He met many people from all parts of Europe, and not once was anyone racist towards him. He really started to understand what it meant to be European, even if he was originally from the East. My father always left notes around the house, and on one note, it said: *'It is so interesting to note that when I see people from Europe, I see a Caucasian person who belongs to a multitude of diverse cultures. He or she could be from any one of the European countries, from a different background, and all that difference should always be embraced.'*

As time went by, my older sister Sahira was born. She is an amazing human being; a soft, sensitive, fun-loving girl. Her childhood, like mine, was complex. We both ended up in Christian elementary (primary) schools although we are from a mixed faith. My sister is a very sweet person, and while there is always sibling rivalry, she taught all of us the importance of being in the moment and to always listen to the actual words of any child, to value children as much as possible. She taught us about mental health and that everyone suffers from something or the other. She would eventually become a teacher and would teach thousands of children throughout her career. She introduced us to a quote by someone that said, "It takes a village to raise a child," and it is so true. Her reading skills are superb, and she is so well-read; the subject she loves most is how to enrich children's lives, and her favourite author and philosopher is a lady called Hanna Ardent. Sahira truly is a gem.

From the success of the restaurant, my dad invested in two race horses. He named them Ambrose and Hafiz, and both ended up being multiple winners. The day he sold them, he slowly invested in real estate. My dad is a wise man, and he is very good with accounting. His only bad habit is that he loves gambling. At the various casinos and race tracks, my dad used to take me to different cafés and restaurants to try all the different foods and to smell the aroma of fresh croissants every morning. Yummy!

As time passed by, I grew more and more aware that I carried the blood of two very different cultures and faiths, yet I was sent to a Christian all-boys elementary school. I would look into the mirror and I would see a chiseled face, with a pointed nose, white skin, blonde, dusty hair, and one light green eye and one light blue. I have a smile that is contagious, and I could not believe I was growing up so fast. How could I be a blonde, blue-eyed Muslim? That truly rattled my brain as well!

I used to have long conversations with my parents about their upbringing and their diverse faiths. I was curious to know, as I looked like any other European 10-year-old, yet I had parents from 2 different religions and I was attending an English private school called Saint Mary's in France! I really needed to know who I truly am.

I always asked my parents why they decided to get married if they are both from different races and faith backgrounds.

They both laughed and said, "Love, and it is purely for the excitement!" They just kept on laughing and hugging. Yuck!

At 10 years old, one day, my dad woke me up in the middle of the night. He asked me to wake up, as he had a dream about losing me and he wanted to speak to me immediately.

"Jules, wake up."

"What is it, Papa?"

"Wake up."

"Ok, Papa, hang on."

I tried to get out of bed and fell on the floor!

I began crying, and my mum came running in to find out what happened...

"Jules, are you ok?"

"I don't know. Papa pushed me on the floor!"

"Whaaat? Nooo...I did not do that. Jules, stop lying!" Papa screamed.

"I'm just pulling your leg. Gotcha!" I shouted as I got up off the floor.

They were not amused, and as a punishment, my dad made sure I was wide awake to have a discussion with him there and then in the middle of the night!

"Jules, I want to tell you something. I had a dream where you were falling from a cliff, and you kept on falling deeper and deeper. It woke me up. I just want to let you know that we love you very much," said Papa.

"Can I please go back to bed? I have school tomorrow."

"Not yet, Jules. We need to know that we have

gone through everything with you. You know your values and virtues, yes?"

"Yes, Papa."

"If anything happens to me or Mama, you know what to do, yes?"

"Yes. I should go straight to the King and tell him what happened."

"Jules, all I want for you is to be happy, to be content with life and to know there is a purpose for your life. Remember, Jules, whatever beliefs you have, there is always some sort of problem. To make sure you are fine, always turn to being good, always look to helping others and follow all the religions and faiths that represent good. Will you remember that, Jules?"

"Zzzzzzz…" I was fast asleep. That was my childhood; getting infused with values at any time of the day!

"Awww, Jules!" My parents went back to sleep, shaking their heads.

In the morning, before heading off to school, my mum asked me, "What was Papa talking about last night? What was he saying about beliefs and faith?"

"I am not sure, Mama. I was so sleepy. Can you tell me what he said?"

My mum responded, "All people of faiths, beliefs and religions are like raindrops dropping in different places of the world, but eventually, these raindrops merge into a stream that merges into the ocean. We are all raindrops inside, and our ultimate goal is to go on this journey and merge with this ocean called God. Jules, the more you know yourself, the more you know God."

I am still confused by that statement from her.

I reflected on that statement from her for the next 3 years. As a 13-year-old teenager, it was very important for me to trust my parents' advice in giving me the correct answer. Not only did they give me the right answers, they infused me with so many positive values that I really have a good sense of who I am....

My parents talked to me every night about being a good human, always instilling positive values; not just what they are, but how I should live according to those values. They started teaching me about the relevance of peace, ethics, moral judgment, intellect, empathy, inclusiveness and the dignity of being a human. Sometimes, I would get so tired of listening, but they just kept on advising me so much that most of the advice became part and parcel of my DNA!

Fortunately, we all had a great life through their hard work and prudence. Living in Europe had its fair share of excitement, and one fine day, my parents made a life-altering decision. King Rumi Khan identified Africa as a continent of opportunity. He advised us that, though it would be a long, winding road to eventual success, it would be a continent for personal success for generations to come. I am sure there were some other reasons as well, but parents keep secrets from their kids when they are young, I guess. After much due diligence and researching new opportunities, with the constant guidance of the king looking into Africa as a potential continent to derive new sources of income, our family decided to move to a British colonial country called Kenya in Eastern Africa.

2

The First Attack

MY FAMILY SOLD our business and properties in France. They invested in my mum's new JK Boutique custom tailoring clothing store on Government Road in Kenya's capital, Nairobi, and in my dad's real estate business, which was based in Lavington, Nairobi. It was exciting to be a part of the move, but I truly felt my parents were uprooting their lives based on an uncertain economic future for our family.

Life in Nairobi, the capital of Kenya, was blissful, filled with new perspectives such as servants, cars, money and beautiful people. My mother and father were such a loving couple, and both were so perfect to me.

I am always grateful that I was blessed with amazing parents that are so gentle and kind, generous, and caring, and who are always sharing their knowledge with others. All I knew is when I grew up, I wanted to work on the values that my parents represented.

Sunday is the best day of the week for me, the day of rest, as Christians say. Sunday is family day for us, and my parents would always call me into the kitchen to have a private discussion after lunch was over.

This particular Sunday, my parents shocked the living daylights out of me by revealing a secret beyond my belief!

"Jules, it is time for our one-on-one discussion with you alone. Please come into the kitchen and ask everyone to leave us alone."

I kindly requested everyone else leave the kitchen, and that they close and lock the door behind them, because it was time to have my parental discussion of the week.

"Jules, you know we love you?" my mum started.

"Yes, of course, Mama," I replied.

"You know I stitch clothes for a living, yes?" she went on.

"And you know I manage and build homes for a living," Papa said.

"Yes, of course Papa, but you know I really have a lot of homework today, and to be honest, you and Mama never really discuss your work with me. Is that what we will discuss now?" I asked.

"Ahh," Mama said.

"Mmm," Papa said

"Well, Jules, as my son and as your mother, I have to admit to something that needs to be discussed. You have come of age, and…"

"Noooo, Mama!" I cut her off. "I am not going to hear about the birds and bees from you two!" I shrieked.

They both began to laugh and giggle, and I thought I needed to get out of there fast before they grossed me out….

"Jules, it is not the time to talk about the birds and the bees, but if you want to, I can," my mum said to me calmly. "However, what I have to say is far more important. I have to admit to keeping a secret from you for a very long time, a secret that can put all our lives in danger." Mama looked at me with deep concentration.

"Mama, stop being so serious," I replied.

"Jules, I have to tell you that Papa and I, in addition to our normal working lives, we are…." She hesitated, and I began to tilt my head and frown a little in confusion.

"We have been entrusted to protect an ancient book from the past, a book that has been written by a Prophet of God. We are sworn to protect this book with our lives; it's a book that can assist humanity today and into the future." Mama blurted it all out so quickly, and then she looked at Papa to continue the conversation.

"Mama and I are secret caretakers of this ancient book, and, as caretakers, we need to defend the people of the book and to ensure that the book never ever gets into the hands of evil." Papa was so serious that I knew they were not joking around. "In order to protect this book, Mama and I were trained by the king and his army on how to defend ourselves through the rigorous practice of ancient martial arts mixed with assassin weapon training." Papa was now standing so close to me that I began to squint my eyes to really grasp what was going on here and now.

"Your Mama and I do not hurt people unless, and only unless, it is in self-defense. Not only is this a family secret, but it is a family tradition that goes back many years," Papa said.

I looked at Mama; she was staring right at me, just waiting for my response.

"What the h..." I stopped before the swear word came out.

"Hey, no poor language, please, or we will wash your mouth with soap!" Papa yelled.

"Yuck, Papa! You guys are just lying, yes? There is no way two of the most boring...ah, I mean, most down-to-earth parents are assassins. Is this a joke?"

I really did not believe them, and as a teenager, I thought my parents were trying to act cool and were just pulling my leg. There was no way my two picture-perfect parents were assassins. I found them quite boring, if I may say so myself.

"Jules, Jules, Jules," my mum said, while shaking her head. She picked up a kitchen knife and threw it at my father. I looked at the knife as it flew in slow motion from her hand and into the middle of my father's outstretched palms; he actually caught the knife between both his palms and, with a circular motion, stabbed the apple that was on the table!

I fainted, bumping my head as I fell to the ground, and when I came to, my mum was pouring some water on my face. I sat up as I regained consciousness (I have a low tolerance if anything happens to my parents and people I know, so I generally faint, which is really embarrassing). "Jules, wake up, wake up." My mum was shaking me and cradling me, making sure I was fine.

"You guys are kidding me, right?" I asked.

Both my parents started to giggle!

"You guys are kidding me, right?" I asked again.

"Jules, my boy…it is time to tell you the truth," my mum said.

The three of us sat there on the floor, and my mum began to narrate a parable of our early European ancestors, who lived in a mountain village located in the Alps in Sweden.

She started, "During World War One, our small village was about to go under a severe attack by a larger neighboring enemy army. We were located high in the mountains, and the invading army was planning their ruthless attack from the base of the mountain. We could see hundreds of flickering camp fires coming from their camp. The largest camp fires came from the enemy king's tent. At night, the village elders sent a beautiful maiden to the enemy king's chambers. This maiden was from our family, a well-trained assassin; she was, of course, scared, frightened, alone, and hardly dressed for being out so late at night, yet she went unescorted into the king's tent. Immediately, the king told everyone to leave him alone to be with the beautiful maiden. As they sat to eat some dinner, the King forcefully grabbed the maiden's arm; the maiden quickly splashed wine into his eyes and knocked him out with a swift knee-kick to his head. While he was unconscious, the maiden carved a small, deep cut on his upper right cheekbone. In the morning, when he woke up, she was gone, and his eyes and cut were bandaged up really neatly. The beautiful maiden had left him a note by his bedside, secured by a very sharp dagger, that said, *'Dear King, I apologize for meeting you in such a deceitful way, and as much as it hurts me to have to hurt you, imagine what our entire village will do to your army when they go to sleep every night!'* The king told his army to fall out and never return to what he called the 'mountain full of assassins'! Thus, our family history, Jules!"

"Holy moly, are you telling me the truth?" I replied.

My mum looked me up and down. "Do I ever lie to you?"

My mum began to tell me, "Papa and I cannot take care of you all our lives, and before the age of 16, we would need to know that you can take care of yourself."

I was no more than 13 years old when we reached Kenya, and my parents were gearing me up for full-on independence!

My mum explained, "We are a family of secret assassins, and as protectors of a mysterious, ancient book, it is our duty to invest in your education and see that your education would not be an ordinary one," she explained. "In addition to secular school education, we will teach you a value system that every child needs to be taught. We will teach you to look at the world as a beautiful pearl, and not as an earth divided by man-made borders. People will always go to war for some silly political reason, and they would blame these political reasons on racial, faith or economic differences. If we do not educate and protect this earth, who will?"

She broke the news that I would be attending a boarding school from that moment until I turned 18, and that the boarding school was a world-renowned school because it was the world's only secret teenage assassin boarding school.

"Holy macaroni! Mum!" I screamed.

My mum went on to explain, "King Rumi is actually your grandfather, and he sent us to Kenya to protect this mysterious book while making sure we could run our business successfully. This book is currently in the East African region of the world." She continued, "When your dad arrived in France, he did not mention that his family came with him. As poor as your grandfather was in India, he was the King of the Refugees. Once your grandfather arrived in France with your dad, he began to build his empire."

I understood now that not only did my family keep secrets from me, but that I was really messed up! Was I an assassin or a prince?

My Mum went onto to explain further. "In case the mysterious book moves, we have to move as well. It may not be the same country, but we will be very close by. Only your grandfather and his network know where the mysterious book is at any given time; it is an empire built of members from diverse faiths."

I asked my mum, "As a family, are we looked upon as bad people as Muslims?"

She replied, "Jules, the first rule is never begin to overgeneralize a faith, a culture or a tradition. Never assume that all the people who belong to a faith are all the same. We are all different and unique, which means what I am about to tell you is the way we as a family perceive our personal heritage, so I am not speaking about all Muslims, Jewish or Christians, as there is too much difference within every faith itself. The way we live should make others realize that Judaism, Christianity, Islam or any other belief structure contains so many various traditions, and that the majority of all human families are all peaceful and are made up of very different traditions and civilizations." She continued, "Each of these civilizations has a diverse culture and people of intellect never overgeneralize." My mum proclaimed, "Everyone breathes the same air, everyone eats the same food, everyone chases the same dollars, and we are all a mixture of peaceful civilizations; everyone is the custodian of the air that we all breathe. A person of belief in God is someone who follows God's gracious commands and should act as a support to every other person on this planet, regardless of someone's race, faith or civilization. We are all one human species, and we need to look after each other. That's why we look after this book. The book," she whispered, "contains the secret to everlasting peace."

I asked her, "Why do they keep on moving this mysterious book all over the world?"

Her reply was simple. "It is a secret." She explained, "Our family has the burden and responsibility of protecting this mysterious book, and in order to ensure the book and humanity's safety, Jules Khan, you will need to learn how to protect yourself and others."

I replied in a very thoughtful voice. "Mum, why should we take this burden on? Why can't the world just fix itself, and we can all live in peace?"

She responded, "Jules, in life, you may not think you have been chosen to do anything, but if you look at every teenager, you'll realize that each teenager has been blessed with so many talents. It is up to them to realize what they want to become and how to use their God-given talents and put them to use throughout their lives." I was still a little upset at the fact that we had to disrupt our lives over other people we did not even know!

She hugged me and told me, "Jules, I love you, but it is time to leave for a journey of a lifetime. Try your best at the boarding school. I know you will, and that's all I want from you."

I left the capital city of Nairobi on a colonial steam rail road train. I waved goodbye to my parents as my family sent me to the finest self-defense assassin boarding school on the outskirts of Mombasa, located on the south coast of Kenya.

I was sad in one way, yet really happy that I was travelling on my own for the very first time. As the train began to move, I looked for my room, and it was in first class. That was great, but it had bunk beds, and I wondered who was going to be in the room with me. As I sat there arranging my bags, a man knocked on my door and asked for my ticket. I turned to my bags, and he suddenly grabbed me violently around the neck and started to choke me!

I tried to get free, but I felt as if I was dying. I blacked out, and the next thing I knew I found myself lying on the floor next to the man who had attacked me. I was baffled and did not know what had happened. Just then, the staff came in, followed by a lady who said her name was Mary and that she was my older sister.

I said, "She is not my older sister!"

She just laughed and instructed the staff to dispose of the man lying on the floor. I was shocked; it was like a movie! I had experienced someone almost kill me, and then my saviors were going to take this assailant and probably throw him off the train! I fainted again and woke up a few hours later.

Mary was staring at me while I rubbed my eyes. I asked her, "Who are you really?"

She replied, "I work for your mum, and she sent me on the train a few minutes after you boarded. She told me someone would probably try to kidnap you or harm you because your family protects the mysterious book."

Still confused, I asked, "What did you do with that bad guy?"

"None of your business, kiddo," she replied.

The train travelled non-stop for 12 hours, cutting through small villages and game parks. I looked outside the window and felt the air passing through my hair and on my face. Kenya is a truly magnificent country, I thought. The beauty lies in its nature and its smiling people. It was dinner time, and the young African bell boy came by to ring the bell for guests to attend the evening meal.

I looked at Mary and asked her, "Will you please join me for dinner?"

She replied, "You go ahead and meet me after for cookies and milk. My room is right next door to yours, and if you need anything, simply knock three times, and I will know it's you."

I got dressed in my three-piece black tuxedo, white crisp dress shirt and black bow tie and walked to the dining room. It was so majestic; there was silver cutlery and white linen tablecloths, and my eyes were mesmerized with the table setting. Placed in the middle of the table was a candle lit inside a glass lamp. The lamp was pearly white and shined like a star on the table, the candle lit by a small bowl of some mysterious, luminous oil.

As I sat down, the waiter gave me the menu and waited until I decided what to eat. He told me, "This is a 7-course meal, and you should take time in choosing your selection. You can eat as much as you want to."

"I will try a little of everything," I told him, and he went off and started bringing me the best meal I have ever tasted in my life!

After dinner, I knocked on Mary's door and asked if she would like to have some coffee together. She said, "You are too young for coffee, but I will join you for some milk and cookies."

I said, "Sure."

Mary and I sat in the dining room and

chatted about life. She told me that I was in a lot of danger, as the National Weapons Association would kidnap me and try to get to the book. "The National Weapons Association is so wealthy that they can bribe any official to get to your parents and you. Your mum's instructions were crystal clear… 'Take anyone out that even comes close to harming Jules.'"

We arrived in Mombasa at 5:45am while the sun was just rising. What a beautiful sight it was as the train arrived through hundreds of towering palm trees and hundreds of people!

Mary knocked three times, and I knew it was her. She asked me if I was fine and told me she would take me to the boarding school. We travelled for another two hours in a classic Model T Ford until we got to the South Coast of Mombasa.

3

Assassins Boarding School

THE DRIVE WAS really nice. We left the train station with both Mary and myself sitting in the back; the heavily armed driver and co-driver kept an eye out for anything suspicious. We drove from the train station through the town of Mombasa. What a wonderful place Mombasa was! One could see the impact of the British Colonialism at its peak, with replica buildings from the United Kingdom planted in the middle of an African Arab city. There were so many Churches, Temples, Mosques and JamatKhana's that I thought, wow. This is a hotbed for cultures and faiths under colonial rule. As we drove past the town and headed towards the South coast, we stopped to fill up with some gasoline and were met by some local Africans selling us fresh coconut juice, sugar cane sticks and delicious apple mangoes.

Mary and I could not stop eating and drinking. Although she was a few years older than me, we both got along really well. She was a mentor that I would come to respect and value throughout my life.

We arrived at a palm-tree-lined farm deep in the South; on one side was this farm, and on the other side I could see the vast beautiful beach and Indian Ocean. The gates were solid steel and camouflaged by bushes and trees. The driver approached the gate and spoke to the guard, and within a few minutes, an army of guards surrounded the car.

We were told to enter and walk the remaining way towards the school. Mary and I left our luggage in the car and were escorted by guards all the way to the main reception.

The boarding school was an old Portuguese fortress, and the architecture was nothing I had ever seen or read about. The closest I could think of was a Spanish Gothic Villa, if there is such a description; lots of sand-colored slabs and brilliant red, green, maroon, and yellow stained glass with images of heaven. 'A grande fortaleza,' or simply, 'fortaleza,' was printed on the fortress doors.

The grand fortress doors opened, and the headmaster, Mr. Charles Massey, and the staff came to greet Mary and myself.

Mr. Massey began to explain a little about the school. "The boarding school is surprisingly run jointly by the elite Jewish, Arab, Maasai, Indian, Chinese and United States special forces stationed in Mombasa. That is serious diversity! This assassin school was initially founded by the Maasai tribe of Eastern Africa. The Maasai are known to be able to kill a lion with their bare hands or a simple shield and javelin. The Maasai are well known as nomads, yet what is so fascinating about them is that they do not recognize borders, countries or fences. Their first priority is their cattle, and wherever their cattle want to graze, that's home. The Maasai follow the laws of nature and not the laws of man, something all humans need to learn."

Mr. Massey went on. "The school was set up during the time of Colonial invasions in Africa. A few of the elite soldiers broke away from their various countries' armies and built this secret assassin school for the protection of humanity, and not just for the protection of one government or one ideology."

Mr. Massey looked at Mary and said, "Thank you, Mary, for delivering Master Jules safely to us. We will take him from here."

I turned to Mary and gave her a tight hug, then waved goodbye after thanking her for saving my life on the train. I decided at that moment that, respectfully, I was going to be the best assassin this school would ever have!

Mr. Massey took me for a tour of the school. It had sand-colored walls and gothic looking architecture lined by deep red and purple velvet curtains to keep the sunlight out; there were very strange lit up niches with golden candles inside every wall, lit by the same mysterious luminous oil as the lamps on the train. As we walked deeper into the fortress, we entered an area that was so quiet. At the entrance of the door, I looked up and I read what it said: *'Ye who enter here, enter humbly and leave here as a master of the Epistles.'*

I asked Mr. Massey, "Sir, may I ask what this word means? 'Epistles?'"

He replied, "Jules, many years ago, around the 8th Century, a secret organization was based in the deep East around Persia somewhere. Men, women and children decided to preserve the latest knowledge of the time. Back then, it was difficult to store knowledge anywhere. Therefore, the majority of knowledge was simply memorized, and everything was literally stored in people's minds. When civilizations were able to obtain any form of writing materials or ink, they would do so to prioritize the preservation of knowledge at any cost. Many advanced leaders from all over Persia tried preservation, but to no avail. Then, one small esoteric community led by their king came up with an 'intellectual preservation strategy.' This secret organization developed a system whereby there are four sections of developing Masters. They believed that when a human is born, he or she is born a Master. As these Masters grow and advance intellectually, they move through these 4 stages. The first stage is Adolescenthood, the second stage is Adulthood, the third stage is Masterhood, and the fourth and final Stage is Prophethood. The Secret Sect invited all humans who possessed higher learnings to begin documenting all that humans have learned over the years. These documents were then separated into sections, just like encyclopedias. Today, there are 52 Epistles that contain facts, thoughts, research, and intelligence of the known and the unknown world of knowledge. After all, knowledge is light, or enlightenment! Therefore, as you spend the next four years here, you will master each of the 52 Epistles and what is contained in them. By the time you leave 'Fortaleza,' we would have attempted to cover most of the intellect of the human mind and spirit. So, in essence, Jules, you have 52 subjects to master in order to graduate!"

As we walked past each classroom, or Epistle, we saw some of the kids in their classrooms and walking in the hallways. They all had uniforms that matched the Epistle they were learning; complete immersion, if you ask me. I was so mesmerized by the connectivity of the building's architecture, design and ambience and how it connected to the students' demeanors. They all seemed so calm, relaxed, happy and focused.

As we toured the fortress, a group of boys and girls approached me to say hello. I greeted them, and Mr. Massey introduced them to me and said, "Jules, let me introduce you to the most powerful assassins the school has ever had. This is Reeshma, Mimi, Samuel, Rickson, Julie and Ahmad."

My heart sank. Just a few minutes ago, I told myself I would be the best, and here in front of me were six of the best.

I asked the boys and girls if they could take me on the rest of the tour, as long as it was okay with the headmaster. Mr. Massey agreed, and they took me on a tour of the entire fortress. The kids were really nice, and I thought, wow, I don't need to beat them, I will just join them!

I settled into the Boys' dorm with the rest of the boys and kept my things neatly. There was a room for every child, and I changed my clothes, brushed and flossed my teeth, combed my hair, and washed my face. Before I fell asleep, I would say my nighttime prayer:

"Oh, Lord, I bow my head in humility, I softly fold my hands and ask for your kind forgiveness; please accept these prayers. In the name of God, the most beneficent, the most merciful, all praise is due to you, the one and only almighty. Our Father, who art in heaven, hallowed be thy name. Thy kingdom come. Thy will be done, on earth as it is in heaven. Give us this day our daily bread, and forgive us our trespasses, as we forgive those who trespass against us, and lead us not into temptation, but deliver us from evil. Thank you, Lord, for all that you do for everyone and everything. Please look after everyone, especially the small animals Good Night."

I jumped into bed and was out like a light!

My daily routine at the boarding school was unlike any other education on the planet. Let me give you just a small glimpse into my daily schedule:

Splash! Cold water was thrown on my face at 3:30am – yikes, what a wake-up call! All the students were woken up every day by 3:45am. We were taught methodologies in meditation for 15 minutes, and we would then meditate for an hour, then power yoga for an hour. Finally, there was a gourmet breakfast of food that was grown on the grounds of the fortress and cooked by the students. Then, we would shower and get dressed in our uniforms and go off to our respective Epistle class till noon. The students ate lunch either in the grand hall or alone on the grounds; it was our choice. Lunch was prepared by the students again, and everything was uniquely vegetarian for lunch. After lunch, specific assassin training went on until 3pm. The training was lethal, intellectual and painful. The students would then break for snacks and resume humanities education from 4pm to 6pm. After, the students would learn multi-faith prayers and multiple languages from all cultures from 6pm to 9pm. The students would eat a light meal between 7pm and 8pm, normally Spanish tapas. Then, from 9.30pm to midnight, the students and teachers would have deep conversations on philosophy; we would debate on how we should improve humanity and all that resides on the planet. Lights out at 12:30 and up again at 3:30am!

The classes were never really held indoors. The school was on such a vast property, with sprawling gardens, streams, rivers and the ocean all playing a vital role in the way we all lived and operated within the 1100 acres.

At Fortaleza, I learned how to use ancient

undiscovered martial arts. They taught me to use everyday objects I came across and convert them into self-defense instruments of injury. Unlike my parents, who would sing pop songs while bashing people, I chose to recite prayers from diverse cultures, translating them from their languages into English while I bashed my bad guys! The assassin boarding school taught us not to kill, but to instead disable the assailant so that they would never want to harm anyone during their lifetime.

The training was fascinating. Every day, we learned something new, and it had one main focus: how to use intellectual force to create peace. We learned so many traditional strategies that averted the loss of life, and we were re-taught simple concepts, such as the true origins of chess; how empires decided to use strategy games as opposed to simply going into war to avoid mass casualties. We were taught to think about the greatness of humanity and how preserving this humanity is as important as preserving the planet. Our combat training was all guerilla warfare and how one person could take out more than 10 to 12 enemies with movements that all the students had to master. The training was so intensive and rigorous that by the end of the night, we would all be flat!

After one whole year of training, there was an announcement on the PA for the top eight students to enter a combat mission with a teacher. I was shocked when I heard, "Jules Khan to the combat room on the roof now."

As we entered training, Mr. Massey took over the class.

"Today, kids, you will face a final Phase 1 combat situation. There are 4 combat phases throughout your stay here, and this phase is one of the most difficult psychologically and physically. Please do not hold back, as the students that pass this round will enter into the advanced level. All you need to do is try and take me down individually, and not as a group."

One by one, he threw us to the ground and kept on shouting at us to get up and fight like an assassin and not a warrior. For three solid hours, he went at us non-stop. As the fighting got more intensive, Mr. Massey screamed and said, "Look around you; look around the room use whatever object you can find and attack me!" Most of the eight students, including myself, were either bruised or seriously in pain. I thought, what the hallelujah is going on? The only way I could take Mr. Massey would be with some sort of weapon.

I looked around, and I found a broom and snapped it in half and began attacking him! He casually threw me to the ground, and then I'd had enough! Enough of being thrown around, enough of this nonsense; most of the eight students were rolling around in pain. I decided to take out a prayer because I felt guilty… I knew I was going to injure my headmaster…

"Mr. Massey?"

"What is it, boy?" he asked.

"Can I go and get a glass of water?" I replied.

He was furious. He ran towards me to give me a slap, and I kneeled down as if to say sorry. As he slowed down his approach, I thrust the broken broom stick through his shoe laces! He screamed in agony and, as he was looking down at his foot, before he could pull away I raised my body and knocked him out with a head butt. He fell like a chopped log and landed with a 'thud.'

There lay Mr. Massey, unconscious and bleeding from his foot. We were all shocked, but

I prayed and prayed… "O God, please forgive me. Please let him be ok; I won't do it again…" I prayed and thought I should learn some better prayers than just, 'O God, please forgive me.' I promised myself that from now on, I would research as many prayers as possible! I quickly told the other kids to get some ice, bandages and masking tape.

We placed Mr. Massey on a reclining chair. I removed the broken broom from his bleeding foot and elevated his leg, bandaged him up, and then subsequently taped him to the chair in case he attacked us again!

The vice principal came in and made sure he was fine, then she cleaned his wound quite thoroughly. She said, "I have never seen Mr. Massey wounded like this; maybe this will teach him a lesson not to fight with the kids too early."

The vice principal asked which junior master was able to do this, and I raised my hand. She smiled and said, "You, my dear, have an assassin's gift. Go ahead and take the afternoon off. Take a walk around the school, and I will make sure Mr. Massey realizes that you are ready for advanced training. You will not be in trouble and, in fact, the administration will ensure this in writing.

Once you get back in the evening, we will meet and discuss further. Run along, everyone. Class is cancelled for the rest of the day thanks to Jules Khan."

I ran out of the room and kept on running until I reached the edge of the cliff near the river. I stopped to catch my breath, and I started thinking about where life was going to take me and how much I missed my parents. I felt bad about what I did, but I thought to myself that the training was a little rough, and the only way I could defeat him was to injure and then knock Mr. Massey out without killing him. As tears rolled down my face, I cried relentlessly, not holding back. Who says big boys don't cry? Well, I was a big boy, and I was crying like a baby.

As I walked further and further away from the school, I came across an area that was out-of-bounds. There was a raging river below, and I had heard that many people had fallen from this cliff, so I was pretty careful. I looked across, and it seemed there were a couple of people on the opposite side, a man and a woman, and they were talking to each other. I moved closer and closer to have a better look, and I slipped! Luckily, I held onto the edge, but I could hear the raging river 100 feet below! I felt myself slipping, and my fingers could hardly carry my weight. "O God, please don't let me die today, I promise, I promise." Then, suddenly, I slipped some more and dug my face into the cliff while I hung on for dear life… "Oh God, please, please save me. I will accept any burden you give me!"

Suddenly, I heard a voice calmly and firmly saying to me: "Do not look down. Do not look down."

I tried to lift myself, but I could not climb up. I was slipping and hanging on with every shred of energy I had! Suddenly, I heard the voice again saying, "Do not look down." Just then, I felt as if Mother Nature put her arms around me, and I felt the wet mud, grass and roots encasing my body. She began pulling my entire body up onto the cliff.

What the halleluiah was happening to me was freaking unbelievable! As I tried to move, I felt a strange, painful sensation all over my entire body. I could not believe my feelings and my eyes… roots, water and soil were piercing and entering my entire body from all my pores; from every conceivable opening of my body, these elements of Nature were pouring into me! I screamed in agony. I felt as if I was being violated by Mother Nature; she was literally filling me up with earth. I began to sweat; the pain was so severe as every inch of me was filled with roots, water and soil, and, as usual, I fainted. It must have been hours of this happening, and yet the worst was not over...

I woke up engulfed inside the cliff. I looked around, moving like a human inside of Mother Nature, like an embryo inside a womb. I swirled from one side to another. I could see, I could breathe, I could drink water, I could pee, I could poo, I could live inside here. I thought to myself, what the hallelujah is going on? Suddenly, I felt a cramp, then another, and another; holy Father! Contraction time, I know what that means... time to go through excruciating pain and be born! "NOOOOOOOOO, God, please, no more pain!" The next contraction was really violent! I felt as if I was bursting inside, and then all of sudden water from all directions, jelly-type water, surrounded me. It felt like some sort of plasma – God's creations are amazing, I thought to myself. We have so much to discover as humans. As I became more resilient to the pain, which was like nothing that I had ever encountered, I noticed this gel seemed to be luminescent and full of knowledge. It felt as if this plasma was made up of liquid neurons. I could hear movements in the soil, I could feel the worms looking for water, I could hear a fox dig his burrow, I could feel a crow pecking for worms… I was in Earth, creation, heaven; whatever this was, it was mind blowing. I started talking to myself, saying, "God is constantly creating, and we are constantly discovering his creation. This creation is infinite and simply outstanding."

I was now comfortable inside Mother Nature. I was still receiving contraction shocks, but I was aware, I was so aware that I felt one with Nature – there was no separation. Suddenly, after three violent contractions, my head was facing downwards, my legs were stretched, and I was pushed violently through roots. I was shooting down to Earth's core at lightning speed, and I felt as if my skin was tearing off; burning off is the correct description! As I travelled further down, I realized I was heading toward the middle or the core of the Earth. It was beautiful, luminescent and very colorful; the minerals I went through were glowing, round dots alone, but together, they created different shapes and sizes. Just like written words, I thought to myself. "Everything starts with a dot, and then as you write, you make different letters and images." I was truly experiencing Nirvana.

As I was bolted through the Earth's crust and then through the Earth's mantle layers, I heard voices, voices that I imagined came from advanced humans who were called 'Spiritual Masters.' They told me not to worry, and that this was my destiny; to share my experience with others, and that God's creation is not limited to simply diversity of race but to diversity of creation. When all creation makes an effort to work together, the closer we all get to God's love.

As I continued descending into the Earth's core, I felt a melting sensation, as if I had turned into hot, molten lava. I was immersed in an ocean of water and unbearable heat. I realized that, as humans, we are made up of water, minerals, heat and God's hidden love. Inside Earth, it is so beautiful. Just like the sky full of stars, inside Earth, it is full of brilliant undiscovered energy and minerals.

Humans simply have to dig deeper and they will discover energy that can benefit this universe!

I thought to myself that I felt as if I was outside of my physical body, as if I was as light as air and I felt no pain. As humans, I thought we needed to redirect our focus from making weapons to creating energy. At that moment, I knew my purpose in life! To get everyone to move from fear to hope, to make governments and people invest in energy instead of weapons.

Speaking of weapons, I was face down and being dipped in hot, molten lava; I felt like an ice cream getting dipped in hot chocolate. I was then spun around in the hot lava and brought facing upwards. Contractions began again, but this time, the contractions were more like cannons, busting into me and forcing me upwards! I flew from the core into the mantle then up into the crust, and as I looked around, I could see my human form coming back. Eventually, I burst through a few feet from where I originally was cliff hanging. I was hurled through the earth and landed hard, heavy with mud, water and roots coming out of my naked body! Yuck, I thought to myself!

I lay there in the hot sun and said to myself, "Creation is from God's love for humanity; he created Earth for us to learn, and God created diversity in all forms only in order to discover more of God's unbelievable creation."

I began to feel dizzy, cold, and scared, and I simply blacked out. I had no idea how long I had been lying there.

As the pain subsided, I awoke dazed and was leaning backwards. I looked at the roots flowing right into my arms, and it was as if the roots were holding my hands and the Earth had created a cocoon around my back, protecting me. I tried to lift myself and, to my amazement, I knew I had gained Superhero strength; I just knew that what I had experienced was real and that God had gifted me with powers from Mother Nature. This was surreal, almost like a dream, but this was no damn dream: this was real. I was literally lifting myself in slow motion. I pulled myself forward and got up, but I knew I was not the one who helped me up. It must have been something mysterious. I was covered in mud, water and roots, and the only thing I could think about was that Mother Nature wanted to strengthen me. She was helping me because she knew I was going to help humanity, and I would protect Nature from human destruction. I remembered my mum teaching me about the North American First Nations people and how they knew that the spirit existed in everything. This was definitely one of those surreal moments when Nature's spirit saved me!

I believe this was the point when I received my Superhero powers. After that day, my reflexes became lightning fast and I could slow down time in my mind to complete any task. Day by day, as we took time to translate ancient prayers into English, my powers would suddenly start; they kept developing and getting stronger as my teenage youth passed by. I would find myself researching my superpowers, and they were intertwined with Mother Nature's powers of Earth, Wind, and Water. They were also tied in with the natural human body becoming supernatural. I could travel through soil, roots, and trees as long as they were connected, just like a railway system. I could enter water the same way from one city, travel through earth and oceans, and emerge into another city, state or country in a millionth of a second.

As I tried to fly, I was so disappointed, but I

tried and failed miserably. I knew I was one with the wind, and finally, one fine day, I travelled through the highest tree I could find. I came to the last leaf, where I would normally return down, but this time I focused and pushed myself out off the leaf and found myself standing there at the top of the tree! I screamed with joy, "Yes, Yes, oh God, yes!!" I was so excited, I began to fall. As I crashed through the branches and heard cracking sounds, I started to pray: "Do not take the Lord's name in vain; call unto him only when you need to and when you want to praise him!" I stuck my hand out and forced my hand into the pores of the branches and slid inside. Yeah, baby, that's what I'm talking about!

I travelled and travelled all over the world, including the United States, from New York to California. As I landed, I started to practice my powers at Fortaleza... I could throw further, I could run faster, I could jump higher, I felt as if my mind would ride the wind, I could hear noises a mile away, and I could throw a javelin with pin point accuracy; every year, I could throw further and further. I could see microscopically, and I felt invincible...the only thing I could not do was fly! However, I could appear through the trees, leaves, earth, water and wind, which I thought was a heck of a lot better than simply flying! I would conquer flying one day, I told myself.

I would always relate to Nature. Whether it was moving as fast as the wind or throwing items as fast as a lightning bolt, the development was ongoing. I had no idea how powerful I was getting, but whenever I would think of an enemy target, all I could replicate was the physical pain the previous Prophets and their followers suffered. All I knew was when I prayed in English, I would trigger these Superhero powers.

The funny part was, I could travel into Earth through a tree, but when I came out, my clothes were all torn off and I was covered in roots! Yes, buck naked and covered in mud!

I had to figure this out, as it was getting really embarrassing every time I tried to hide and enter school. One night, I called my mum to figure this out.

"Hi, Mama, how are you?"

"I'm fine, Jules. The question is, how are you?"

"How is Papa?"

"He is fine. The question is, how are you doing? Is anything wrong? You never call me."

"Mama, we are working on a secret scientific program, and I am the test subject. Imagine if I could be buried underground naked, and I could travel 10 feet under the ground and then emerge from a fox hole…" I hated lying to my mother; it would burn me up… I continued, "Imagine, if I could travel in the roots and emerge from a fox hole and I was getting shot at with real bullets or even worse. What kind of clothing would you be able to custom make for me, if that was the case?"

"Hmmm, Jules, that is so interesting. Give me a few months and I will have something that you can wear instead of any underwear."

Six months later, my mum sent me a Superhero suit! She called it the Jules Khan one-piece Super Suit. She had guessed what I was able to do. In any case, she sent me a suit that resembled a two-piece well-fitted New York stockbroker business suit, with a white shirt and burgundy tie. It felt like I was wearing spandex with millions of small, soft scales, which felt odd. It looked like a mix of linen and spandex, and it also looked like a wool suit; it was bullet and shrapnel proof as well as waterproof, and on the neck, I could pull out the head cover. It even came with a built-in soft, transparent cover for my face.

I would wear my Jules Khan Super Suit under my normal clothes, and when I travelled through Earth, I would remove my clothes and have my Super Suit on.

I still needed to figure out how to remove the dirt from my hair and face. Yes, there was an opening for me to do my number 1 and 2 (just in case you wanted to know!).

Any time a school opponent faced me, I would start my prayers, initiating my Superhero powers, and I would injure my opponent with pin point accuracy. Many times, I thought of Jesus and the pain he went through for all of us.

As the years went by, I grew into a confident, caring, empathetic young man. I would take long walks through Mombasa, meeting people and listening to their trials and tribulations, although I could not do anything except take out prayers that life would improve for them and all of us.

Mr. Massey was always nice to me after the injury, although he walked with a walking stick permanently. He would always thank me for not harming him further. He said, "Teachers need to work with their students and not against their students." He was grateful, as opposed to being mean and rude. He always taught me the philosophy of good against evil and that good will always prevail, even if it has to be a little harsh!

It was now 1943. I had just turned 18 and was ready to leave my private boarding school in Kenya for Harvard University. As a family, we made a long-term decision to move our entire family from Kenya to New York City because we knew the mysterious ancient book was now in North America, hidden in some museum. My mum had travelled to New York a year earlier and opened her boutique bespoke clothing store, called 'JK Bespoke Custom Tailoring.'

My dad and I left Mombasa, and we spoke at length on the plane that brought us to London's Aerodrome. We caught a famous black taxi from the airport, stopping over in Wembley Central for a short family visit. The cab dropped us to my great aunt's house, located at 64 Station Grove in Wembley. How I loved that house, I thought to myself. As I spent time in United Kingdom, I loved Oxford Square, Bond Street and Piccadilly Circus. I loved shopping there and walking around looking at everyone. London used to be a place of such class, with an air of excellent mannerisms. In the future, I could see it would become a serious melting pot of technology and humanoid robotics – scary!

As we finished our short family visit and boarded the American Airlines plane for New York, my dad spoke about the shortness of this material life and that we should start concentrating more on the spiritual life. This was always hard for him, he said. Later on in life, I would notice that he worked tirelessly at trying to settle down in New York City, but it was difficult for him – going from living a life of luxury in Kenya to having to do everything ourselves. It was a difficult adjustment for him for sure, but he did manage to purchase an old Manhattan brownstone house and began renovating and selling properties. His fortune kept on growing as the years passed by, yet he was not happy in New York compared to India or Kenya. I realized in life that if you have everything, you have nothing, and if you have nothing, you have everything. Life is such an illusion, I thought to myself.

4

Harvard University

A S A FAMILY, we were advised by King Rumi Khan to seek the best education and to keep on being educated throughout our lives. I frantically searched for universities to attend. Many of the boarding school students would choose universities that were game changers in society. I started searching for the oldest universities on the planet. It was a tough decision between Oxford University, and its history with Rhodes Scholarships; Al-Azhar University in Cairo, one of the first universities established in the Fatimid Empire and known for its multiple historical discoveries; or Harvard University, as one of the oldest universities that had an established Law program. I knew I was going to pursue Law, and my parents insisted that it was non-negotiable that I had to be in a university on the East Coast of the USA.

Fortunately, on my end, I aced Harvard's entrance exam and knew what Harvard Admissions were looking for. They were not looking for the next millionaire; they were looking for the next savior of humanity. As long as you had a social purpose and excellent grades and you could afford the university fees at Harvard, they would welcome you with open arms. Harvard University has a healthy endowment fund, and I took full advantage of researching their scholarship requirements. Luckily, I received a full scholarship for my studies at Harvard, and my ambition was to specialize in Ethics and Law with a focus on humans settling in space one day.

My interview at Harvard was stressful. Facing what looked like a panel of old bearded wizards in double breasted suits, the questions kept on coming without any remorse.

The professors' interview questions tore into me one by one:

"As a mixed blood, why do you think you fit into this prestigious university?" one asked.

I replied, "As humans, we are all mixed blood; one clot from the male and one clot from the female. Where this blood comes from or where it originated from, I do not know, but what I do know is that I am here today wanting to use Harvard's intelligence to pursue Ethical Law. One day, this will support the advancement and conduct of human beings wherever they live. These humans, I assume, will be of mixed blood as well."

"Mmm," was the response from the professors.

"If you had to choose between the USA and France, which one would you call home?" another asked.

I replied, "Home is where the heart is. My mum taught me early on that it is man who creates borders and borderlines. My home is where there is shelter, where Nature takes me, and how I treat my neighbors. Whether I am a citizen of France or the United States, I consider myself a citizen of humanity."

"Mmm," was the response from the professors.

"At Harvard, we speak Latin or English, and we are glad to see that you speak so many ancient languages as well as English. Which language do you consider more superior?"

I responded, "Language is only a form of communication. Whether I speak multiple languages or consider one better than the other is irrelevant. What is relevant is that I have the tools to communicate, and whether I communicate in English, Latin or Mandarin, the responsibility lies upon me to be respectful, thoughtful and empathetic to everyone I communicate with because traditions and languages are to be built upon. So, for me, respectful communication is the superior one."

"Mmm," was the response from the professors.

"Next question: do you believe in God?"

I replied, "Yes, I do. I understand that many people have their own beliefs, and I respect that. I also respect and accept the various religions, but at the end of the day, we are all here on a spiritual journey, and I fully intend to live in this journey moment by moment. The fact that I do not know how we all came into existence and how the clouds form or the sun shines every day is nothing but a sign that God is ever-present."

"Mmm," was the response from the professors.

"Last question: what faith do you belong to?"

"Ahh, this one is easy," I replied. "Faith is belief, and I believe in the Almighty Lord; he is the same Lord all the Prophets believe in. The faith I belong to is one that believes in one God, the acceptance of all religions, the sanctity of life, and the dignity of everything that has been created. I belong to a faith of peace, humility, respect, intelligence, and the acceptance of the Lord. So, in answer to your question, I may be termed Muslim, Jewish, Christian or other, but I am a human, and I belong to the human faith of being God's humble servant."

"Mmm," was the response from the professors.

After 30 minutes of intensive deliberation, the professors stood up and left one by one towards the door. The last professor stood up, looked me in the eye, and said, "Welcome to Harvard, young man."

My entrance into Harvard was awesome. What a beautiful university campus it is, with buildings lined with red brick and manicured green gardens! I received my Harvard uniform and jacket, and I looked at the emblem and read: *VERITAS, Christo et Ecclesiae'*, which meant

Truth for Christ and Church. Well, it did not hurt that I was brought up in a Christian Elementary School...or maybe Harvard admissions thought I was part of the future Superheroes! If I were to be portrayed as a Superhero, I would know exactly how I would appear...I would be wearing my bullet-proof JK navy blue slim suit, a white crisp shirt, a burgundy tie, deep blue socks and brown leather business shoes. I would be clean-shaven and European looking with blond hair, green/blue eyes and a killer body! My superpowers? Using normal human assassin powers with everyday objects as weapons, all while saying diverse prayers in English and leaving my victims feeling the pain of past Prophets and their followers. (Peace be upon the Prophets and their followers.)

As I entered Harvard University, I fell in love. There were beautiful people from all over the world. They were all shapes and sizes, and whether they thought they were overweight, underweight, tall or short, able or unable, they were all beautiful at the university, and I could not keep myself from staring. This was probably my favorite pastime, watching and adoring God's highest creation...people! The students and professors were from all parts of the world, from different cultures and civilizations, and you could not guess who was from where. All I knew was that so many of them were attending Harvard University to improve the world!

As my classes began and I settled into my dormitory, I met my two roommates, Klaus and Angelina. Klaus was from Germany. He was a typical German, I thought to myself; he had a thick German accent, brown hair, blue eyes, and was very pale. I introduced myself right away.

"Hi, my name is Jules. How are you? And what is your name, kind sir?"

"My name is Klaus, and I am fine."

"Klaus, nice to meet you. First year, I presume? And what is your major?" I asked.

Klaus responded, "My reason for being in Harvard is to solve the transportation problem in Germany."

I said, "It is so funny that you want to attend Harvard to solve a traffic problem."

Klaus laughed. He said, "No, you radical. I

want to solve the traffic problem when we have millions of flying crafts 10 feet above us!"

Radical? That was the first time I had heard that word. I thought radicals were those who went against the norm. I was simply trying to fit in!

Angelina was as beautiful as her name. She reminded me of a scientist, for some reason.

I turned to her and started speaking. "Hi, my name is…"

"I know!" she quipped.

"What is your reason for attending Harvard?"

"Mine, dear Jules, is a search for a concrete solution to preserving disappearing civilizations because, in the future, humans and robots will sadly merge into hybrids and eradicate natural human civilizations. In China, we are many people, but we come from endless different villages, cultures and traditions, as well as multiple faiths, and I see all of that disappearing in every race and culture – so I simply want to find unique ways to preserve civilizations."

The three of us sat together and spoke for hours, until it was time to have dinner in the Grand Hall. We changed into our Harvard suits and headed out.

Angelina, Klaus and I walked from our dorm; we had to cross Harvard Square and follow its lush gardens towards the Grand Dining Hall. While we were so engrossed in our talking, five very strong, well-dressed men approached us. One was an American, one was a Russian, one was Chinese, one was German, and the other was French. How ironic, I thought to myself, that these 5 men represented the very same countries that were gearing up to export the most weapons in the world in the future. I moved aside, and before I knew it, one had struck me on the head with an iron pole. I fell to the ground bleeding, and I was about to faint when I saw Klaus land some heavy Kung Fu moves on the four assailants. Down they went, one by one. I got up slowly, and Klaus pushed me under the bushes and told me to keep still.

The Harvard security guards came running up to find out what happened, and all of a sudden, they too began attacking Klaus. From nowhere, I saw Angelina take down two of the guards like Catwoman! When she finished with them, she looked at me to check on my status. Klaus made sure none of the assailants got up, and he was ruthless, breaking either their ankle or wrist. He told them, "If you ever come near us, you will not be alive. Send a message back to your kind bosses that we are coming for them soon."

I was in total shock. What was happening? This was my first day at Harvard University, and there was a whole lot of butt-kicking going on in Harvard Square!

5

The Mystery In New York

KLAUS, ANGELINA AND I got back to the
dorm, and all I could do was wash
the blood off my face. My head was
pounding, and when I closed my eyes, I felt the
room spinning; damn! I had a severe headache.
I locked the bathroom door and quickly jumped
into the shower, but as I turned the taps on, I
heard Angelina scream "Owww!" outside the
bathroom. She screamed again and said, "Jules,
get out here!"

(Yes my parents named me Jules Khan – what
were they thinking?) I pulled on my Lacoste
boxers and opened the bathroom door only to get

punched in the face. I saw Angelina struggling and wrestling with an assailant, and Klaus was being tackled by two assailants. Why was I calling them assailants, and why the hallelujah were they after us?

I knew it was time to use my powers, and it was not going to be pretty...

I started slowing everything down in my mind and began my prayers. "Our Father, who art in heaven, hallowed be thy name, thy kingdom come, thy will be done..." As I continued my prayers, I picked up my belt that I had left on the desk and two sharp pencils as well. I leaped into the air and whipped the assailant who was attacking Angelina. Before he could move, Angelina knocked him out cold.

I continued, "Our Father, who art in heaven, hallowed be thy name," and I stuck a pencil in the middle of the next assailant's palm and pinned him to the desk; I stuck the other pencil in and did the same to his other palm. I continued, "The Lord gave his spiritual child to humanity and He gave us eternal life... O heavenly Father, forgive me, for I have sinned." I knocked the assailant out with a swift knee-kick to his chin.

I looked around to help Angelina and Klaus,

but they had already hammered their assailants into concussions.

Klaus, Angelina, myself, and all the knocked-out assailants were lying there in silence for quite a while. I asked Klaus and Angelina, "What the hallelujah was going on?" Klaus and Angelina both were in pain, but they slowly started laughing and crying so hard that I could not help but do the same. As we got up, I said, "I have to finish my shower and wipe the blood off my 8-pack!" The laughing continued, and I took a long, well-deserved hot shower!

I finished showering and walked out with my body wrapped in towels. I found the dorm room surprisingly cleaned up, with Klaus and Angelina sipping a cup of Boston's best dark roast coffee. Klaus and Angelina had a body clean-up service at Harvard University, for sure!

I went to my room and got dressed in my crisp white shirt, Harvard tie and navy double-breasted blue suit that my mum tailored for me, and I joined Klaus and Angelina for a coffee. As I sat down next to Klaus and Angelina, I looked at the cutlery, which read: *The property of Her Majesty, the Queen of Pluralism.*

I turned to Angelina, and we started to have quite the conversation.

"Angelina, if I may ask, who is Her Majesty, the Queen of Pluralism?" I wanted to know.

She replied, "We are not sure. All we know is that she speaks to us through telegraphs or the phone and pays us for protecting high-level targets. She has kept a provision of 4 years of fees to keep a watch over you until you complete your degree; however, we have received a phone call that you will not be able to complete your degree at Harvard and that we have new instructions. In the event you die or disappear, the fees cease to us, and the fees cease in the event she calls us and relieves us of our duty at any given point in time. So, you see, Jules, this is not an easy lifestyle, getting paid for protecting others, but when you find your purpose in life, then everything becomes a whole lot more enjoyable."

"So, you have never met this Queen or her family before?" I asked.

"Never. We have no clue who the Queen is, but like I said, when you find your purpose and you get paid to protect that purpose, then it is acceptable and enjoyable. I did have a very long discussion on the phone with the Queen before I took the assignment of protecting you. Her Majesty spoke to me about taking on the assignment of protecting a mysterious ancient book and the one person who will bring realization and further peace on Earth, especially after what we witnessed – the sad loss of so many lives in World War I, and now here we are, back in World War II."

I reflected on what Angelina was telling me, and I started to realize that if there is a chance to help prevent and stop wars, then I am up for that job 24 hours a day and seven days a week.

Angelina went on to say, "Klaus and I will be protecting a very young and capable student at Harvard University, and that young gentleman's name is Jules Khan, or you. We need to take you to this ancient and mysterious book if anything happens to the Queen. She told me the book is always protected in a museum, but which museum it is hidden in, we have no idea. However, we need to look after you at Harvard until we get further instructions."

"Wow," I replied.

"Yes, Jules, this is one hell of a ride with you," Angelina quipped.

As I looked down at the cutlery again and focused on the word *Pluralism*, I looked deeply into her eyes and asked her another question. "Angelina, excuse me if I sound a little immature, but what is the meaning of Pluralism?"

"Water," she replied.

I frowned and shook my head. "Water?"

Angelina smiled and said, "That is exactly the same reaction I had when Her Majesty explained it to me on the phone before we took the assignment of protecting you. Her Majesty said, think of the word 'water.' Is it singular or plural?"

I was silent. I could not decide if it was singular or plural…!

Angelina laughed and said, "See…puzzling, huh? Her Majesty also laughed with me and told me not to worry, but to simply reflect on what I was about to hear. She went on to explain what Pluralism is, and I am sure she did the same with Klaus… The Queen said, 'Imagine, on an average day, it is raining outside and you are able to look at each rain drop individually. You will find that they are similar to humans. Take, for instance, how they all come in different shapes and sizes; they are made up of water, but inside them there is dust, minerals or what we call the core or nuclei. Within each raindrop, when light passes through them, they create a prism of colors. Just like humans, we all have the light of God, but we come in different races and cultures. The rain drops naturally connect with each other as they fall through the sky, and they split again to continue their own journey, just like a family. But when these individual rain drops reach the ground, they have their own individual journey to go on. Some raindrops simply evaporate, some feed plants, some gather and create a pool of water, some find streams or lakes, and some end up in the ocean, but at the end of the day, when these raindrops reach Earth, each one has a purpose. When these raindrops gather together to create a body of water, they are more effective than a simple singular raindrop."'

Angelina was so intense as she continued. "Her Majesty then explained that humans are like raindrops, all different, and Pluralism is like water; when all the raindrops get together, like when all humans get together and work together using their diversity, then there is a better result for everything."

I was quiet for the longest time. This was the first time in my teenage life that anyone had explained what Pluralism is. How we, as humans, are dependent on each other and using each other's differences to come together and enjoy God's creation; to be part of God's journey, all while improving humanity! I was enlightened, and I reassured myself that I was on the right path of believing in God and the success of humanity.

Klaus had just finished speaking to someone on the phone, and he looked at me and said, "Let us pack our bags; we have to go to New York City before we all get killed here. Let's go rent some fast cars and get out of here."

"Why New York? I still have to finish my degree! I just got here today," I protested.

Klaus responded, "You came to Harvard, and the very first day you were nearly dead, so I think you will have to finish your degree when we know things have settled down. No one is telling you to stop your life-long education."

I asked, "Why New York?"

Klaus laughed. "Jules, you do not know? New

York is the epicenter of the New World. Yes, there are lots of museums to keep the mysterious ancient book safe, but New York is the birthplace of the New World. With the recent failure and collapse of the League of Nations, the world is looking for lessons learned and best practices to start up another world body to ensure that we do not have another World War. The world is setting up a new council; we think it is called the United Nations Council, or something like that. Jules, the world needs leadership. Humans will need leadership, and sometimes the most effective leadership is secret leadership. Imagine a world where we are led by people who have no interest in their personal gain or ego. The United Nations Council also has secret leaders, and these leaders that have proven to be the most effective are what we secretly call the 'Gills,' just like the gills of a fish. These leaders that are in the Gills Council are the same ones that are at war with the National Weapons Association. These special secret leaders in the Gills Council are made up of different leaders from all over the world."

"But what does 'Gills' mean?" I asked, puzzled.

"'Gills' stands for 'Guide in Light, Leadership, Service.' These leaders are like the raindrops

Angelina explained to you; just like a raindrop has its purpose, it is the raindrops that realize they have the light of God inside of them and that this light guides them into leadership for the services of humanity. Heavy, right?" Klaus asked.

I replied, "Yes, that's heavy enough for a teenager, but it is good that you made me realize that this planet ain't working on autopilot, and all of us have a purpose. Both of you have made me realize the importance and success of Pluralism."

"You got that right, kiddo. It's time to rent those cars, and the last one to New York is a rotten egg!" Angelina added.

6

Heading To Jerusalem

WE RAN TO the only private Independent European vehicle rental agency located near Harvard University; it had been set up by a Mr. Heindrick Hans, a recent Harvard graduate. One good thing was that Harvard had one of the wealthiest student bodies in the USA, and so renting exotic cars was very easy: simply give your student number and sign a promissory note with interest against your fees, and you were good to rent any vehicle as long as you had a valid driver's license and could pay for extra insurance!

As we entered the rental agency, Klaus looked over the cars and asked, "Which one, Angelina?"

She replied, "BMW 328 only!"

Klaus laughed and asked, "Jules, which car?"

I replied, "Ferrari, if that's an option."

Klaus looked at the lady clerk and she said, "Yes, we have one; an 815 sport."

"We will take that one as well," Klaus responded. He then said, "I would prefer to go with the Rolls Royce, please."

The clerk replied by handing us all the documentation, and once it was completed, we were shown the vehicles and subsequently drove off.

As we headed to the airport, I drove my Ferrari 815 Sport, followed by Angelina's BMW 328 and Klaus' Rolls Royce. The three of us were racing each other like fools and out-pacing the police. We finally were caught by Boston's finest. Klaus got out and showed them his card, and they issued us with speeding tickets and a warning. I asked Klaus, "Who are you two?"

"I'll tell you once we get to Manhattan," Klaus said.

Our destination was the Waldorf Astoria. As we entered Manhattan, it was everything I had dreamed of: a wealthy 18-year-old, driving a red Ferrari, passing SAKS FIFTH Avenue and then eventually entering the parking lot of the Waldorf Astoria.

The three of us parked our respective cars in the hotel VIP parking, and we all got out. I said, "I am not moving until you tell me what's going on. How did we get past those policemen?"

Angelina began to move closer to me; she was simply beautiful. She turned to me and said, "Klaus and I were to protect you at Harvard University while you completed your Ethics and Law degree. We are your family's employees and the best assassins on the planet. Due to your family's contacts, we have diplomatic immunity wherever we go. However, since the attacks on you at Harvard University, we have been ordered to move you to Manhattan pending further instructions. Is that good enough for you?"

Klaus turned to me and asked, "Jules, where did you learn to fight?"

I replied, "Klaus, as a young boy, I was sent to a self-defense assassin boarding school in Kenya." I explained the day I acquired my superpowers and that, while at the school, I also learned multiple prayers, especially the prayers of the three faiths from the Book. I learned Judaism, Christianity, and Islam, I learned how to meditate as a Buddhist, and I read a lot of religious texts from the world's major religions; as I recited the prayers, I somehow transformed into someone who could slow down time and events in my mind. The prayers would elevate my powers and inflict surgical pain towards my opponents, and any pain was reminiscent of any pain God's Prophets or their followers went through. "Peace be upon them and their families," I added. "I have been blessed with superpowers that are still developing, as I am still in disbelief that I have these superpowers."

"Yeah, right. Baloney!" Angelina said.

"I do not believe you have superpowers, Jules, but I do believe you have been trained exceptionally well," Klaus added.

I was hoping they would believe me, but seeing is believing I guess!

I turned to them and asked, "Can you share with me how you became assassins and where you guys were trained?"

Angelina looked at me sternly, and then she just kind of relaxed and started. "I was left in an orphanage in Beijing, China. I have no clue who my parents are; the orphanage is my family. While I was growing up in the orphanage, I was taught that no one would look after me except me. I would play, work and train every day, as resting or wasting my time was my enemy. At the orphanage, we had to look after ourselves and help the new babies that were dropped off every morning. One morning, when I was 9 years old, a baby was left at the main door. When I went to pick it up, it had already passed away from the night's cold. I looked across the road and saw a teenager looking at me, and I felt she was the mother. I walked up to her with her baby and I asked her why she would do this…she cried and held her baby, then started to tell me her story:

"'My name is Anna, and I was taken hostage by some men. They would not feed me, and they would make me slave for them until I gave birth to my baby. When my baby was born, those evil men told me to throw it in the garbage, but my child was stillborn and had already passed on.'

"She wept and wept and kept on kissing her baby's forehead. I took them both into the orphanage, and both of us prayed and buried the baby boy in the backyard. I found myself obsessed and kept on asking for more and more details on those men that had kidnapped her."

Angelina continued, "Finally, after a year, I summoned the courage to go to the village with Anna and track and kill those who had harmed Anna and her baby. Anna told me where to find those evil men and what they looked like. Both Anna and I stayed at her friend's house in the village, and we kept on looking everywhere for these men. After several days of searching, we found all four of them at the local drinking house. Anna was very frightened when we saw them, and I told her to go back home and wait for me. As midnight approached, I went up to them at the bar and called out to them… 'Hey, boys, want to have some fun?' I asked. They immediately began to run after me, so I ran outside, where they trapped me by surrounding me on all sides and took me to a room in the back of the bar. Before they could do anything, I asked them why they do what they do."

"They all laughed, and one of them replied,

'We are evil and have no value for life. Any time we can kidnap someone, we will use them like slaves, and tonight it is your turn.'"

Angelina went on.

"They thought I was small and timid, and as one of them reached for me, I pulled out my homemade weapon... I stabbed him in the stomach with my long, thin knife laced with lethal poison. He laughed, but then started throwing up and realized he was about to die. The second man came to catch me, and I slit his throat with the knife. As he fell to the ground screaming, the other two men raced at me, and I let them grab my legs. All I had to do as the next man grabbed me was puncture the skin with my poisoned knife; down the 3rd man went. The fourth man dug his nails into my leg, and I plunged the knife deep into his right eyeball." Angelina was quiet as she was recalling her ordeal. Finally, she began again. "I looked around at these four vile creatures that were lying dead on the floor and thought to myself, I actually feel good. I feel like some sort of retribution angel. I did, however, take a prayer out to Jesus Christ to give them their rightful punishment and to look after their innocent families, if they had any."

Angelina was now pacing up and down as she continued. "When I got back to the orphanage covered in blood, the teachers washed me up and asked me if I was fine. I told them I had never felt so good in my life. I hugged my big adopted sister and told her we must leave in search of an assassin or army school. The headmaster of our orphanage was an ex-army man, and he said he would train us to become China's best assassins and we could stay at the orphanage as long as we liked, as he wanted us to know that not all men are evil. As my training progressed and I grew up as one of China's number one assassins, I wanted a break. I ended up in the USA as an immigrant to further my education. I studied at various local colleges, moving from one college to another until I met Professor Andreas. He knew my story and referred me to the US Secret Service. I trained with them for over three years and decided to quit when I found out that a few of their top officials were corrupt; although many of their top officials were honest, I was not interested in their politics. Ever since then, I have been working for anyone who is willing to pay top dollar; I do not kill for money, but I now protect for hire."

"Wow, Angelina, that's so cool! Not the part

about your upbringing, but the part about how you prefer to protect someone as opposed to knocking people off," Klaus said.

Angelina shrugged her head and said, "I prefer protecting lives now and not simply taking them."

Klaus started, "My story is a lot different than yours or Angelina's. I was born in Berlin, Germany, and all I knew was either pre-war or post-war, when I never wanted to be born in any war. My family was very happy. We all grew up on a farm with animals. My dad was a genius at fixing all the machinery at the farm. He had a part-time job as well at the weapons factory in the evenings, and every morning I would find spare parts that were considered unusable by the German army, whether it was a piece of metal, broken screwdriver, etc. We used to have a smelter at one of the barns in our farm, and I would spend all day melting the items my dad brought from the weapons factory. Slowly, as time went by, I would mold and shape very sharp pieces to throw at targets, items like the ancient ninja shuriken, which was a 4-sided ninja star. I loved making the ninja stars, but I could never throw them and make them stick in a target. One day, my dad advised me that he read in one of his school books that the Japanese did not throw the ninja star or shuriken; they would hold it and use it in close combat.

"I told him that was very cool and I would modify it to become a close-range weapon.

"He said, 'Good luck; just have fun,' as he closed the door behind me. I suddenly heard some gunshots and screaming! It came from my brother's room. I ran towards the house and my brother's room, and there my brother was on the floor with what seemed to be a bullet wound to his heart. My mum was screaming and crying."

"Then what happened?" both Angelina and I asked.

"I heard another loud gunshot and saw my dad drop to the ground, dead. There was another gunshot, and I saw my mother drop to the ground, also dead. I crawled under some furniture and made my way to the living room. There were three men in ski masks in the room, and one of them kicked me in the stomach and asked for any money or valuables that we might have. I asked the assailants why they needed to kill my family. They responded by saying, 'We will even kill you; just give us the keys to the safe.' I said, 'Which keys?' They responded, 'The keys to the safe that is hidden away in your dad's bedroom.'

"I said, 'Let me go look for them,' and I ran to the barn and collected all my ninja stars and tucked them into my pockets. As I returned from the barn, one of the assailants was waiting for me while the other assailants were on the balcony. As I approached the first assailant, I reached into my pocket and asked him to come closer. He obliged, and when he got near me, I stuck two ninja blades into his neck. He screamed in agony, and I took off as fast as I could. I jumped out the window and landed on the hay stack. I ran under the house and between the barns, and I avoided all their gun shots. I ran to my uncle's house, which is a mile away, only to find them dead as well. I mustered up the courage to cover their faces with bed sheets and hid there the entire night. In the morning, I woke up and realized I had just lost my entire family."

Klaus had a few tears running down his cheeks. He continued:

"I hardly slept all night in fear of these guys attacking me; combined with the freezing cold and crying all night, I was really messed up. As I looked at the bodies of my extended family, I decided to walk back home to see if those devils had left. As I slowly approached my house, I could see a small fire burning outside, and I heard voices. I hid behind the small shrubs and crawled closer and closer to my home, all the while thinking and hoping my family would be alive."

Klaus was crying now, and I was not sure he should continue, so I interrupted. "Klaus, you need not go on any further."

Klaus was silent for a while as tears dropped down from his eyes onto the floor. He then continued again. "As I crawled closer and closer, I could smell the burning of human bodies. They were burning my family. I clasped my hands around my mouth so that they could not hear me. I was so angry, and I said to myself, I have to kill these guys. I summoned my courage and crawled to our shed, where I found a pitch fork and screwdrivers. I stuffed all of the screwdrivers into my pockets and sat in the shed thinking, what I should do? Before I could do anything, one of the assailants kicked the door open, and to my shock, it was my neighbor! What the hell! I thought to myself, why would they want to do that?

"Before I could think, the assailant ran towards me screaming, and I raised and plunged the pitchfork into his chest. He screamed in agony as blood splattered everywhere. The next thing I knew, three more of my neighbors came in looking at me as I stood over the body of their father. They rushed to capture me, and one by one I stabbed them either in their groin, stomach, neck or face. I was a ruthless killing machine; nothing was going to stop me from eliminating these guys after what they had done to my family. Once I finished with the four neighbors, I knew there was one more left, and he took off like any other coward would. As I stood there, I heard more and more screams, and I looked up to see what was going on. It was terrible…neighbors were turning against neighbors…this new fascist ideology was tearing our German fabric apart."

"Days passed. I had buried what was left of my family, and I began to look after the home. None of my family members were left; all were dead. One fine day, a German soldier not older than 20 knocked on my door. He was injured and collapsed in front of the house. I heard more voices, so I moved him away from the door and pulled him to the bushes to make sure he was camouflaged. As we hid under the bushes, three Army men started shouting and saying, 'Boris, if we find you, we will kill you for deserting the German Elite Army!' I saw the three soldiers go into my house, then they set it on fire and left."

Klaus continued, "I sat there one more time and watched everything I owned going up in flames. I asked myself, why? Suddenly, the soldier woke up in a sweat and grabbed my arm as if to protect me.

"He looked up at me and asked, 'Are you ok?' I laughed and said, 'Yes, I'm fine. I saved you, Boris!'

"Boris replied, 'How do you know my name? Did those soldiers come after me?'

"'Yes,' I told him, 'they did.'

"'What is your name?' Boris asked me, and I told him, 'Klaus.'

"Boris was very slow when he spoke. 'I'm sorry, Klaus, for your loss, but our country is losing their minds and we have neighbors killing each other.'

"'Boris, can you teach me how to fight? Can you teach me how to never be scared or intimidated by anyone?'

"'Klaus, as long as you promise me that whoever you kill attacks you first, not the other way around, yes. As Germans, we need to protect our values and civilization, as well as humanity.'

"'Yes, I promise,' I told Boris.

"That's my story, guys. Boris is like my older brother and keeper; he taught me everything I needed to know about assassins. It was not long before I got recruited by the German Army, and not the Fascist one. Throughout my employment with the German Army, I helped save lives as opposed to taking lives."

"WOW!" Angelina said.

We were quiet for a moment. An awkward silence fell upon us while the three of us were thinking of our pasts. Then, out of the blue, *bang, bang, bang, bang, bang, bang!* Gunshots started to ring out. Klaus was hit in the chest, and Angelina was hit on her thigh. Angelina pulled out a canister and threw it, letting it spew red smoke all around us. I followed her as we dragged Klaus into the BMW and took off as we heard more gunshots.

As we drove out, I looked at her and Klaus, but both had not sustained any major injuries. "Simple bruising. Your mum's tailor-made suits are life savers for us."

I looked down at their suits and noticed for the very first time they each had a very faint "JK", and then inside the suits I saw "Jules Khan Bespoke Clothing." It was the same brand I had grown up with all my life. I thought it was my mum just having fun and stitching the brand and the labels inside my daily clothes...not knowing my childhood clothes were all bullet-proof!

Angelina was driving like there was no tomorrow while Klaus was screaming in agony, as one of the bullets had grazed his right hand. I bandaged his hand with a cloth I found in the car, and the blood began to clot.

I told Klaus, "Hold this firmly to stop the bleeding."

Angelina started talking to Klaus in German, and I wanted to know what was going on. Angelina finally spoke in English. "We were given instructions that if you or any one of us are attacked in one country, then we will have to fly out to another one."

I was so confused. What was she talking about? She said, "World War is approaching, and we must get out of New York. The next destination has to be activated, or we will die here. The Queen had instructed us that if anything happens to us in New York, we have to get out of there pronto and head to Jerusalem."

The three of us drove straight to Idlewild Airport. I had read somewhere that they were thinking of renaming this airport the New York International Airport, as the volumes of flights coming in and out were astronomical! As we were driving towards the airport, I saw the Statue of Liberty, and I thought about New York: what a city, what an amazing place! As I thought about the United States of America, I recalled one of the greatest American President's speeches, and it reminded me that President Abraham Lincoln's words were the best: "Our fathers brought forth, on this continent, a new nation, conceived in Liberty, and dedicated to the proposition that all men are created equal." I am not sure why I thought of those words at that moment; maybe because I was thinking about the Statue of Liberty, and maybe the President should have said that all men and women are created equally or that humanity is created equally, but they were inspirational words for sure. We parked the car and headed straight for the airline that would take us to our destination…Jerusalem.

Klaus approached the airline ticket booth and was carrying some sort of letter. As he tore the letter open, three or four gold coins came out. He paid for our flight with these gold coins, and while they looked very different, they were accepted.

We all checked into first-class and were safely on the plane. I slept the whole flight, as I was simply exhausted. I was dreaming of a time when I was young and playing with all the leaves at our house in Kenya. I could feel the cold leaves under my feet while the sun shone all over me. The wind was blowing, and all I could do was smile. It is blissful being a child.

7

Heading To Saudi Arabia

A S WE LANDED and exited the first-class passenger area, we were shuttled through the VIP waiting area and were soon apprehended by the Jewish Secret Service. We were told to wait for the Chief of Security. Klaus asked, "Who is the chief this year?"

"General Moshe," one of the men replied.

I thought to myself, could it be? As the pudgy but confident General entered the room, I shouted, "Doron…Shalom!" We spoke in Hebrew.

He looked up at me and opened his arms. "Jules, you crazy brother of mine!"

I said, "Shalom, my lazy brother. How are you?" We both laughed, as we had known each other since childhood. General Moshe was my childhood friend. We lived in the same neighborhood, called State House, in Nairobi, Kenya. I said, "Doron, I am not sure what's going on. Do you know what this is about?"

Angelina asked, "How do you know each other?"

I replied, "We used to be childhood neighbors in the flats in Nairobi. The first day I met Doron, he was outside in the garden when our neighbor, Bupen, and he were fighting. Bupen sat on Doron's neck, and Doron's mum came out screaming with a broom and hammered Bupen! It was the same technique that I used to take out my headmaster; as soon as I saw the broom that day, I knew I had a weapon that would take him down."

I continued, "Doron and I were in elementary school together with our other two best friends. One Jewish – Doron; one Muslim – me, Jules; one Buddhist – Siddhartha; and one Christian – John. We all used to hang at school all the time. Doron was very advanced in math and science, John was advanced in Law, Siddhartha was a pure dreamer, someone who would only focus on the development of good deeds, and I was really well-versed in discovering God's creations on Earth and in space."

"Oh gosh. Yeah, right, boys will be boys," Angelina replied.

Doron looked at me, then shook his head and said, "Jules, it is good to see you, but I do not have good news for you. However, let's start by letting you know what we know so far about your family…

"Both your mum and dad have disappeared, and the Secret Service thinks they have been abducted. When you left for Harvard University, your parents were taken by the National Weapons Association goons, and we have not heard anything from anyone yet. Your Mother is actually Her Majesty, the Queen of Pluralism, and your father is an immigrant from India. They both secretly work for an organization run by a mystical King. Don't ask me why, but it seems to be something with King Rumi Khan. We hear he is brilliant, and that eventually, he and his heirs will be the bridge between the old world and the new world. Apparently, there was much opposition to your parents' marriage, but both were adamant, and they married; one, a self-appointed future queen, and the other a peasant immigrant who is from royalty.

"Both became successful in their own right and, unbeknown to anyone, including your dad, for his protection, your mum assembled a new, powerful movement. The movement is called pluralism. It is a hard concept, but it stems from King Rumi Khan's belief that recognizes pluralism as a strength for all civil societies. Instead of cultural or faith polarization, they use pluralism as hope and strength. From Kenya, your mother built a secret empire that influences every leader on the planet. Through pluralism and peace, they influence wealth and stability. The evil forces that want to bring them down are the same evil forces that want to keep this world in violent chaos so they can keep on supplying weapons until we all destroy each other. The evil organization is called the National Weapons Association. Your mum has created a positive, formidable global network, and only she has control of this global network. With her kidnapped, her secret organization does not know what to do."

"Doron, how does being here in Jerusalem play a role in where the book or my parents are?" I asked.

Doron replied, "Ahhh, Jules, you still don't understand the brilliance of your mum's moves. She is just like the queen on a chess board, moving anywhere strategically to create peace while conquering her foes."

"What does that mean?" Angelina interjected.

"Her Majesty understands that the past will determine the future," Doron began. "Right now, in Jerusalem, it is pretty peaceful, but she has advised us that this region will bring in decades of uncertainty and violence for the rest of world. She knows that it is not religious beliefs that will bring up walls and security borders, but people's political policies that create divisions and chaos. She knows what we are heading into, that we are destined to create a mess by creating borders on maps and walls when we should actually be looking at natural contours in land and figuring out how humans can travel freely between countries and states. If people or immigrants want to settle down, they need to look to following the values of that country and culture, and if they do not like the values, they must think through whether they want to be in the society or to create or look for a country that accepts diversity. They say there is a country called Canada that seems to be the ideal model and country to follow. Your mother, the Queen, knows that eventually global peace will stem from this region, and that's why we are all working hard in Jerusalem and the Middle East to promote strength of diversity."

All of a sudden, three Army personnel walked up to General Moshe and handed him a telex. He read it intently and looked up at me. "The Secret organization thinks that they have traced your parents to Jeddah, in Saudi Arabia. Luckily, Klaus and Angelina are multi-linguistic and can accompany you; however, we have no Army protection planes currently, and the earliest we can get you on an Army plane is 12 hours from now. I suggest we collect more intel, and in the meantime, we can escort you, Angelina and Klaus to Jerusalem, our Holy City, and ask for blessings from the heads of all the religious leaders from Judaism, Christianity, and Islamic and Buddhist faiths – all of whom want the same thing as everyone else: Peace."

8

Heading To Germany

KLAUS, ANGELINA AND I were escorted by bodyguards throughout Jerusalem. After receiving blessings from various religious leaders, we all caught a few peaceful, quiet moments at the Wailing Wall.

I thought of my parents, the people around me, and the people who I have never met; I prayed for all of their safety and happiness. The three of us were able to pass the house where Jesus Christ grew up. It was very surreal, being in these holy lands where monastic faith took shape.

We then stopped at the house of Jesus Christ and took out some prayers there as well. As we kept on walking, we came across small souvenir-looking shops. As we looked around to buy some items, someone dressed in Jewish Army clothing punched General Moshe in the face; his nose was bleeding and broken, and we all quickly rushed towards General Moshe as his men chased the assailant through the narrow streets of Jerusalem. General Moshe ordered his men to take us out of the situation and get us safely to the airport, and that he would handle the situation from there.

There was never a dull moment on this trip! Off we went to the airport, where we boarded BOAC (British Airways) to Saudi Arabia via Europe. We had to exit in the United Kingdom and then board a Saudi Airlines flight; how archaic, I thought. Why can't everyone just live peacefully and enjoy each other's culture or civilization? I realized my mum was right, that these divisions we see in the world every day are nothing to do with faith, but with simple silly political disagreements instead. If, as one united Earth, we could solve all political conflicts, what a beautiful world it would be. Angelina and

Klaus were already dressed and looking like two typical bodyguards. I looked like any other European, so I knew I would stick out like a sore thumb in a country of my own faith background. How ironic! All of us had passports ready, and I looked down at mine, which said: Jules Khan, Occupation: Student. I laughed and thought, how true. My parents had always insisted I be a student for life and about life!

The plane took off from Heathrow Aerodrome airport toward Saudi Arabia. I was so tired, I fell into deep sleep. During the flight, I woke up suddenly when I felt turbulence and I heard the captain make an announcement in Arabic and English: "Ya Allah…Oh my God." As we approached the Saudi Arabia airport, he mentioned a tense situation, but the plane quickly crash-landed in Jeddah and slid off the runway. Everyone was instructed to get off the plane and run to the VIP lounge. As Klaus, Angelina and I approached the VIP gates, gunfire began to ring out all over the airport. Suddenly, a very large explosion took place, and the three of us were all thrown to the ground. Planes were exploding around us, and I looked up to the sky and prayed, "Oh Lord, have mercy." I saw bullets flying in slow motion across my face and explosions coming from all directions as all of us ran for cover. Angelina and Klaus grabbed me and threw me through the VIP entrance. All of us entered the VIP lounge and began running; there was panic everywhere. As we exited the lounge, Klaus, Angelina and I heard the screaming of little kids from the entrance. I looked up and saw five children with five Saudi Arabian assailants holding them.

"Klaus and Angelina, hand Jules over; the National Weapons Association needs him taken alive in exchange for these kids!" they screamed at us.

Klaus started speaking in Arabic, and the assailants replied in German, "We need Jules! He holds the key to the new world order."

Klaus ordered, "Let the kids go and we will hand him over."

They exchanged gunfire without hesitation, and the kids dove under the chairs. None of the kids were hurt, but the time came for me to pray and protect...

I began to slow down time and approached the assailants at lightning speed…

"O God, you are the light of the heavens and the earth and all that is in-between." As I spoke the words, I found a broken brick from the explosions and picked it up, then threw it towards the first assailant; instantly, he was knocked out! Klaus and Angelina went to work on another two assailants, leaving me with two more.

I began chasing one of them as they fired shots towards my legs. "In the name of God, the most beneficent, the most merciful…all praise is due to God…" I picked up a Coca Cola bottle and threw it towards his head, knocking out assailant number two. I had one more to go. I began my prayer… "All praise is due to God, the Lord of the worlds…" I ran up behind assailant number three and knocked him out with a roundhouse kick.

The kids were safe. Klaus and Angelina had taken their assailants down. The explosions kept on coming, and it just seemed that a war had broken out between Saudi Arabia and another country.

We came across the Elite Saudi forces, and they quickly took the kids to safety. I asked them, "What is going on?"

They replied, "The National Weapons Association is taking down every nation and wants the world to think that all races are at war with each other. This chaos causes weapons sales to increase on every level. Major Omar Amin here…you are Jules Khan?"

"Yes, I am he," I replied.

He grabbed me by the arm and pushed me against the wall…

I looked at him patiently and waited for his next move.

"Your family is tearing my people apart. Your mother is Swedish and Jewish, your father is from Indian and European ancestry and royal Muslim blood flows through his veins, and you look like a European, and you are our savior?"

He went on ranting. "You think that our multitude of tribes and tribal leaders will accept this kind of diversity? You think that we, as the protectors of the Holy Houses, will accept mixed blood?" He pulled out his gun and pointed it at my head.

I responded, "Listen, Major, with all due respect..."

"Shut up, I have not finished speaking." He proceeded to slap me across the face before continuing. "You are a disgrace to the community. You and your family are not true believers; you guys are not fit to be here on this holy land. You..."

I interrupted him once more, this time using my mediation skills. I thank God that my school taught me well when it came to debating and conflict resolution.

"Major, at ease!" I said firmly. "I agree with some of your opinions, that we are on holy land and that I am not a true believer... I am still on my personal journey of figuring out what a true believer is, let alone what he looks like or what his family blood line is.

"I agree that we are standing on holy land, but is this entire planet not holy?" I continued tearing into him while we looked eye to eye. "You may think that looking like an Arab makes you more pious than me, someone who looks like a European. You may think that my parents getting married to someone outside of their community is a crime, but they got married because they loved each other and saw beyond the color of their skin or their faith background."

I was about to finish him with my next statement and change his opinion forever. "You think that you are pure bred? From the blood of Prophets, because you live in the land of Prophets? You truly believe you are higher than all the people in the world that live outside of the Middle East? You believe that God created us to live within our borders and to only marry our own kind? Your belief is outdated."

He looked down at his feet, and then the rest of the forces surrounded me and him.

I continued…

"You think that God created us not to mix? You think that God created us so that we could just be one color and one faith? When God is in infinite creation mode, then why would he listen to man-made rules? Or man-made opinions? God creates and we create, and we as humans are the custodians of the air we breathe, the food we eat, the people we mate and the children we produce. So, Major, the next time you insult my family, you are simply insulting humanity, which also includes your family."

The major looked up and me and said, "I'm

sorry, I was under the false impression that Arabs are the best."

"You, the Jewish, the Christian, and all the religions and tribes who tear humanity apart should now learn that God has created diversity in humans, and we need to respect and nurture this diversity to protect humanity," I went on.

"Omar, my brother, I may look like an American, but my heart is in the holy lands. I would have loved to meet Prophet Moses, Jesus, Muhammad and Buddha, peace be upon them, but we are all one big human family that needs to look after each other." I looked at him, then raised his head and gave him a hug.

"Thank you, Jules. I do apologize; we in the Middle East are so tense, as we feel that the National Weapons Association will rip our culture apart and place an endless war on us just because they want to sell more weapons." He was so sad when saying this.

He proceeded to walk with me, and his Army men followed closely. He began discussing weapons in more detail with me.

"Please forgive me, Jules, for attacking you. The reason I have resentment for Europeans is because they are the main producers for the

National Weapons Association, and they want to divide and conquer all of us in the Middle East. We have reliable sources that there are certain countries in the world that will become the largest producers of weapons, and they will sell their weapons not to their civilians; instead, these industrialized nations will create wars and will sell their weapons to poor nations for decades to come."

"Now you are teaching me," I replied.

"It is not rubbish, Jules. It is happening as we speak. USA, Germany, France, China, India and so many countries will be living in peace and harmony, but they will be supplying arms to countries in this region. They sell, we kill, and they profit," Omar concluded.

I looked around and realized what he was saying was true. Here we were in an airport that was just torn up with weapons made outside of this land…

Just then, General Sultan Saladin came in, pointed at us, and shouted, "Get these three on the Saudi king's private jet to Berlin, Germany; the German Chancellor has asked to see Jules urgently! But first, get them out of here in one piece."

9

My Purpose Discovered

KLAUS, ANGELINA AND I left under heavy protection, and it started becoming clear to me why I was wanted: why some people wanted to kill me and why some wanted to save me. The three of us entered a Saudi Arabian military airbase and boarded the Saudi king's jet to fly towards Berlin. I sat back and started to reflect on my life. I thought back specifically to all the advice from my mum and dad; throughout my life, my parents put me in self-defense assassination classes. My parents taught me multiple languages and traditions. My parents took me to different countries and made me taste different foods. They educated me on so many values, such as integrity, empathy, intellect, moral reasoning, education, unity, generosity, service, human dignity, respect for all individual conscience, quality of life, happiness, and, most importantly, pluralism.

My parents made me believe that there is One God, that there were multiple male and female Prophets and countless revelations; that there are past, present and future spiritual guides, and that these credible guides only want the very best for humanity. They taught me that there is a fusion of the spiritual and material world and both are intertwined, like our DNA. They emphasized humility and that we are all God's servants, and that my duty is to respect my parents as well as anyone else I come across. They taught me how to volunteer and assist whoever, whenever, regardless of race, ethnicity, wealth, poverty or orientation.

My parents showed me that God created all of us, that God wants us to succeed and, as we strive for this success, we ask God for help, and for Him to help others along the way.

⚡

My parents made me mingle with the rich and famous as well as the poor and infamous. Now I knew, as we flew over the streets of Jeddah, that I may hold the key to the new peaceful world.

I reflected on the superpowers I had attained. The fact that I was from a mixed race and mixed faith made me clearly understand that we are all made up of diversity. Even this Earth is made up of diversity, even this universe is made up of diversity, and, really, we all live inside of God's diversity. If I had been granted powers like this, I knew I was the one to save humanity; who else would there be? Why was I even created? I knew then that I was the one.

I knew that I had to unite all cultures, all races, all shapes and sizes, all sexes and humanity to work together to create a peaceful world. I knew what I had to do. I knew we had to crush the culprits, and there was only one way to do this: to value and protect human differences and respect for this diversity. Pure Pluralism.

On the plane, I ended up sitting next to one of the German Chancellor's commanders, and I introduced myself as usual.

"Hi, my name is Jules. What is your name, and what is going on in Germany?"

He replied, "My name is Fredrick, and in Germany, the majority of the Germans do not follow or accept the mad leader at the helm. Instead, they follow the true peaceful Chancellor, and her name is Madame Chancellor Arendt." Fredrick continued, "Chancellor Ardent is a philosopher. The German people do not want to take over the world or want war or violence due to political forces and political greed. Germany has been thrown into this euphoria of taking over the world, which no true German ever wants to do."

The Germans let us land in a secret airbase off the official army grid. There was no way that the internal German resistance was on their own;

there seemed to be a global network of brilliant people working together.

As we landed, I thought to myself that it only made sense. It was the Germans who would lead this peaceful transition. It was the Germans who could put their past behind them and move this planet to peace. Our landing spot was 50 miles from Berlin, and the plane was descending. I looked outside the window and could see plumes of dirt from enemy troops speeding towards the airport.

As the plane landed, everyone disembarked and quickly ran to meet the Chancellor on the airport runway. There were hundreds of her bodyguards and so many of her BMWs all protecting her. She looked tired, but she was so beautiful, I thought to myself; she had jet black hair, olive skin, green eyes and a lovely smile. Her piercing eyes really affected me; it was almost as if she was looking into my soul. Klaus and Angelina were always so close by. If I took one step, Klaus would move to the right of me, and Angelina would move to the left of me. They were always ready for anything.

Chancellor Ardent asked us, "How was your flight?"

Klaus replied, "It was interesting." She began speaking to Klaus in German, asking him to tell the Saudis to leave the airport immediately, as they were expecting the National Weapons Association Army to be there very soon.

Just before Klaus could approach the plane, it exploded into pieces! The National Weapons Association Army had already arrived, firing at the plane and us!

We ran for cover, and it was the first time Klaus left me and protected the Chancellor. Angelina grabbed my hand and ran towards the Chancellor's car. All four of us managed to get into her car and drove off under heavy gun fire. The Chancellor's Army was so smart; they used guerilla tactics to disable the National Weapons Association's onslaught. I watched in amazement as the Chancellor's army used rubber bullets, smoke bombs and laughing gas instead of live ammunition to neutralize any violence.

The Chancellor, her bodyguards, her troops and the three of us sped towards the city center and were finally clear from any chaos; the Chancellor looked at me and finally spoke to me. "I am so happy, Jules. You have arrived just as we need you, and we are heading to the famous Bode

Museum, as I need the codes to open the Arc of the Covenant. We need to read the mysterious book, or this war with the National Weapons Association is not going to end."

I was in shock. I gasped, "The Arc actually exists?"

10

The Arc Of The Covenant

"**Y**ES, IT DOES," the Chancellor replied in her soft yet firm voice.

"What is inside it? And why is it so important to everyone?" I asked to make sure she knew the answer.

She went on to explain. "The Prophet Moses, peace be upon him and his family...Prophet Moses is most probably one of almighty God's favorite Prophets, as Moses gave up his affluent life for his people and to follow God's commands. During this time, Moses led his people from bondage and into freedom, although God knew what was about to happen. Moses left his people and went to speak to God to receive more commands. When Moses removed his shoes and placed his forehead on the dirt to show utmost respect to the Lord, the Lord was annoyed at the chosen people and instructed Moses to take the 10 Commandments, written in stone, so that the people would have a framework to follow in their lives. Moses obliged and realized that humanity needs commandments and guidance from the Lord, because humans are so fragile in their discipline to the Lord."

I asked again, "What is inside the Covenant?"

"Jules, Jules, Jules…" She kept on repeating my name. "The Covenant contains the 10 Commandments, and a mysterious book that is in the Covenant."

"Who is the keeper of the Covenant, and where is it now?" I asked.

The Chancellor hesitated and said, "King Rumi Khan is the mastermind in keeping track of the Covenant, and his followers, which include your mother and father, volunteer to protect the contents of the Covenant with their lives. The King instructs, and all of us follow the instructions to protect the contents; he moves the Covenant from country to country to avoid the

National Weapons Association from acquiring it." The Chancellor looked at me and proclaimed, "Yes, the Covenant really exists, and we need your help."

⚡

At that moment, I had an epiphany, and I knew what I had to do. The feelings I experienced were all surreal. As we drove through the streets of Berlin and raced onto the Island towards the Bode Museum, I was so nervous because I could almost predict what was going to happen.

The Bode Museum had no security guards. It was such a quiet, picturesque museum and setting. We parked and were directed towards the museum. I kept on stopping ever so quickly to admire the magnificent pieces inside the Bode Museum. The museum was out of the world; there were so many artifacts from all over the world. There was so much rich global history here, I thought to myself. I hope all these collections are cherished; there were statues, coins, and artwork. There were pieces of artwork that really affected all of us as we walked deeper into the museum. There were statues of Jesus Christ and

His life, and I thought to myself that Jesus was so magnificent that He gave His life up for all of us to be spiritually free. I thought, even when Jesus was being crucified, He was thinking of humanity, and I remember His prayer from school. It went something like this: "Father, forgive them, for they know not what they do." If it was anyone else, I do not think they would be thinking about others while suffering like Jesus did.

Walking through the museum, I was enlightened. I realized it does not matter who you are, what faith you hold or what you believe; it is how you will treat the next moment of your life. Will it be positive for you and others, or will it be a waste of time for all? I decided it was time for me to do something positive and use what I had been taught all my life…

Fredrick was walking next to me and said, "The National Weapons Association Army captured the Arc in Jerusalem from King Rumi's people and brought it to Berlin; however, Chancellor Ardent and her team had captured the Arc in a daring attack on the German and National Weapons Associations compound in Berlin and moved it secretly to the Bode Museum. To date, no one knows how to open the Covenant."

Somehow, I knew. I knew because it needed the words that my mum, the Queen, had brought me up with.

Fredrick continued. "The Arc of the Covenant is the holy chest that Moses most likely built out of acacia wood and which houses the Ten Commandments."

The Chancellor explained to me, "Inside the Covenant is a special notebook that contains ancient rules to start the process of the new pluralistic world. In the event your mum was kidnapped, you, Jules, are to open the Covenant using a code and hand me this mysterious book that was supposedly resting next to the Ten Commandments." She went on to say, "Jules, we need to open this Covenant at any cost if humanity is to survive the future horrors of the National Weapons Association."

I entered the room at the Bode Museum with the Chancellor, Angelina, Klaus, Fredrick and a company of German guards who guarded the entrance to where the Arc of the Covenant was kept. The room had long, flowing, red velvet curtains and endless beautiful, glowing yellow lamps that lit the room, just like the ones at my school and on the train. It was a very spiritual-feeling room. The Covenant itself was brilliant. It looked like an old wooden crate, ornate, with Aramaic words covering it. The Covenant looked like it had been burnt, cut and abused, but it seemed as if it healed itself…a mystery, in essence, that no one could break into.

⚡

I knew and felt that both the Ten Commandments and the mysterious notebook resided in the Covenant. All I had to do was open the Covenant, look inside, and hand over everything I found to the Chancellor for them to deal with.

I took a deep breath, closed my eyes, and meditated a little. Then, when I felt at peace, I took seven steps to start and started circling around the Covenant seven times, because I thought of the seven heavens coming together to help us. I then recited the Ten Commandments one by one…

11

A New Beginning

I STARTED WHISPERING THE prayers as I walked around the Covenant…
"I am the Lord thy God and heed my Laws…

"Do not replace me with any other God or other, do not take my name in vain, remember the holy day, honor your mother and father, do not kill, do not commit adultery, do not steal, do not lie, do not cheat on others…"

I continued. "The Lord is our God; the Lord is One. Our father, who art in heaven, hallowed be thy name, thy kingdom come, thy will be done on earth as it is in heaven. O God the most beneficent the most merciful, all praise is due to God, the Lord of the Worlds."

The Covenant slowly began to open, as my eyes grew wide, in slow motion. I used an array of prayers, recognizing that even in different prayers, there is strength in plurality. Slowly but surely, that opened the Covenant, and I truly believe love and peace also helped open the Arc.

As I looked inside, I saw the brilliant tablets and felt this mysterious, etched, shimmering and glowing gold writing on the black stones. I started reading the first tablet, and with my hands I began feeling each Commandment one by one. Cold shivers ran through my body as I read each Commandment. This was truly the words of Almighty God; not only his words, but his Commandments. If these were the tablets of Commandments and the bible is the testament and the Koran is the book of principles, I thought to myself, why does society not have religious studies in every school around the world? Why does society shy away from the brilliance of historic, current and future heritages and civilizations? Why can't people, as a global society, embrace this heavenly gift of difference? I placed my hand to my heart and thanked God for this opportunity to be blessed for this realization.

I looked a little to the side and saw a small, leather-bound, tattered book. I did not know if I was imagining it, but it looked as if the book was resting on some sort of soft, golden light. As I picked up the book ever so slightly, the light began to disappear, and I focused on the cover. It seemed to be made of some sort of strong dried palm leaf or sisal. The pages were so fragile that I was scared to damage any of it. As I raised the book out of the Covenant, just then, the Covenant began to close itself slowly; it was miraculous. It became so quiet in the room that I could hear my heart beat.

*

I began reading the book in detail. It was written in Aramaic, with what looked like purple ink, possibly from some extract of a purple flower. I knew how to read Aramaic from school, and I shook my head and thanked my parents for always asking me to pursue knowledge.

The book was so brilliant. It was written so simplistically, with such thought, humility, respect and patience, that I was in tears. I slowly realized that this book was written by two people, and both were the parents of all humanity – I was in shock!

I studied every mark in the book and realized that the language they used included prayers, symbols, and pictures; Aramaic had tremendous reference to the Love for God. I was in total shock that I was reading the book of the Prophets Adam and Eve. It only made sense – who else but the first two chosen humans to let us know what God's purpose was with humanity and how it all connected to Pluralism.

I tried to imagine what Prophets Adam and Eve looked like and how they would have communicated with the Angels or God. How they tried to write down everything they heard, saw or felt, and how they must have felt thinking that what they were writing in this book would guide humanity forever.

I realized what separated humans from all creation…INTELLECT! And here, in front of me, the Prophets Adam and Eve had done what every successful human does: they were documenting their intellect for the benefit of humanity in the future.

I kept on reading the book letter by letter, symbol by symbol, inference by inference and page by page for an hour until I heard a soft voice speak. "What does it say?" the Chancellor asked.

Klaus and Angelina were looking at me in amazement, and I handed the secret book over to the Chancellor. She asked me, "What is inside the Covenant?"

I proclaimed, "The Covenant contains the Word of God – two ancient tablets with the Ten Commandments written on them, and the notebook in your hand is the Book of Adam and Eve; it is the notes of Prophets Adam and Eve, and all that we need to know about God. God's creation is eternal, and we need to use our knowledge to appreciate and understand God's creation. He created us from a single soul and spread us all over the universe so we can understand each other better. That is the way to eternal peace – it is through, knowledge, hope, peace, love and belonging. All this cannot happen unless we embrace diversity. As God's greatest creation, we need to embrace each other and not destroy each other."

I continued. "The Book of Adam and Eve foretells that, eventually, we would no longer be a people of diverse cultures, but one humanity with diverse races and backgrounds. Once we realize that pluralism is what drives human good over human evil and that pluralism will help humanity work with their differences to create new knowledge for solutions, we will taste the beginning of everlasting peace throughout the universe."

The Chancellor began to cry and she began saying, "Your mum was the official keeper of the Book of Adam and Eve, and she had placed it in the Arc; your mum told me the only person who knew how to open this Arc was her son, because he is truth and he lives and breathes in pluralism."

I looked at her and gasped. "Oh, my Lord; my mother and father are no longer alive, are they?"

I began to cry and then, suddenly, hundreds of assailants broke into the museum. We could hear the fighting. We ran from the chambers through a tunnel; a few assailants were guarding the exit, and Klaus, Angelina and I started defending the Chancellor and the book. I slowed down time and began fending off the assailants while reciting one of my favorite ancient Indian Veda: "O Resplendent God! All your servants, your messengers are simply your own manifestations, you are our almighty Father, you are our Mother divine, to you alone do we pray for peace, we are your children forever..."

⚡

The fighting and adventures continue...

Jules Khan
Favorite Prayers

(Excuse any inaccuracies; it's unto you to find
the most accurate prayers- enjoy.)

The Ten Commandments

I am the Lord Your God; you shall have no other gods beside Me. You shall not make for yourself any graven image, nor any manner of likeness, of any thing that is heaven above, or that is in the earth beneath, or that is in the water under the earth. You shall not bow down to them, nor serve them

You shall not take the name of the Lord Your God in vain; for the Lord will not hold him guiltless that takes His name in vain.

Remember the Sabbath, to keep it holy. Six days you shall labor, and do all your work; but the seventh day is a Sabbath unto the Lord Your God, in it you shall not do any manner of work.

Honor your father and your mother, that your days may be long upon the land which the Lord God gives you.

The Ten Commandments

You shall not murder.

You shall not commit adultery.

You shall not steal.

You shall not bear false witness against your neighbor.

You shall not covet your neighbor's house, nor his wife, his man-servant, his maid-servant, nor his ox, nor his ass, nor anything that is your neighbor's.

(EXODUS)

The Lord's Prayer

Our Father who art in heaven,

hallowed be thy name.

Thy kingdom come.

Thy will be done, on earth, as it is in heaven.

Give us this day our daily bread,

and forgive us our trespasses,

as we forgive those who trespass against us,

and lead us not into temptation,

but deliver us from evil.

(Roman Catholic Church)

The Opening Chapter

In the name of God,
the Beneficent, the Merciful

All praise is only God's,
the Lord of the worlds

The Beneficent, the Merciful

Master of the Day of Judgment

Thee alone worship we
and of Thee only we seek help

Guide us O Lord on the Right path

The path of those upon whom
Thou hast bestowed Thy bounties,
not the path of those inflicted with
Thy wrath nor of those gone astray

The Holy Quran

The Earliest Revelation

"O Resplendent God! All your servants, your messengers are simply your own manifestations, you are our almighty Father, you are our Mother divine, to you alone do we pray for peace, we are your children forever...."

The Divine Scriptures

Thank You From the Author:

"I hope you enjoyed
The Adventures of Jules Khan.

I really appreciate and value the fact that you or
someone else bought this book today.

My dream is to see this book as a New York
Times number 1 bestseller, an award winner
in a new category, and hopefully make me a
multi-millionaire!

I would also truly like to see this book become
a Superhero movie and embraced by the
Superhero blockbuster movie houses!

My real reason for this adventure is to help
teenagers and adults learn how to stop the
production of weapons of any kind and to start
the process of embracing human diversity.

We have come from God and we shall return
unto him; can we not return unto Him as a
united, peaceful, and loving humanity?

I leave it for you to positively advocate for
your own life, your family's lives and for your
neighbor's life.

Peace be upon you forever."

The Adventures of Jules Khan

What would you do if you held the power to help the entire world? It sounds intimidating, but one teenager, Jules Khan, embraces his destiny for the good of all mankind and all faiths. Jules takes you on a narrative adventure that spans the globe, which is already raging from WWII, racing against the evil National Weapons Association and their followers. With Mother Nature given superpowers and some surprising and formidable friends, can Jules find out the truth about his family and his future in time to save the world?

Editor's Review

"The Adventures of Jules Khan: A Teenage Muslim Superhero" is a fascinating journey not only across the world, but through one teen's life as he learns about his family's secret past and the role he'll play in trying to hold the world together. While Jules draws his strength from God and prayer, this book focuses on one main theme throughout: respecting all on Earth, regardless of nationality or religion. An excellent book for teenagers and adults alike, Jules will remind everyone of the important things in life.

Rachel Fogg,
Editor Extraordinaire

For more information on 'The Adventures of Jules Khan' visit www.juleskhan.com

ISBN 978-1-9993805-0-2 US$12.99 CAN$16.99

9 781999 380502

Made in the USA
San Bernardino, CA
27 September 2018